To Pat
who always makes
me smile —
Marilyn

LOVE AFTER 70

OTHER BOOKS OF INTEREST

Illness & Grace, Terror & Transformation
Heather Tosteson and Charles D. Brockett, Editors
Wising Up Press, 2007

FAMILIES: The Frontline of Pluralism
Heather Tosteson and Charles D. Brockett, Editors
Wising Up Press, 2008

LOVE AFTER 70

Heather Tosteson
Nancy Pelletier
Megan Krivchenia
Editors

Wising Up Press
Decatur, Georgia

Wising Up Press
P.O. Box 2122
Decatur, GA 30031-2122
www.universaltable.org

Catalogue-in-Publication data is on file with the Library of Congress.
LCCN: 2008934025

Wising Up ISBN-13: 978-0-9796552-4-1

TABLE OF CONTENTS

III. THE REAL STUFF

IV. IN SICKNESS AND HEALTH

V. MOVING ON

HEATHER TOSTESON

FOREWORD

Just how do septuagenarians do it? Joyce Richardson muses in her poem, and the answer is—every way imaginable, and then some. There is a generous sensuality in the work we find here, strong passions, and a sense of surprise at their persistence. If we didn't know most of our writers were over 70, I'm not sure we would think of them that way if we listen to their most personal of voices—which is part of the fun and the invitation of this anthology. Until we get there, we don't know what this age is really like. And until we ask, those who have been there may not volunteer their road maps. But we are the richer, wiser, and more lively for having them.

I remember twenty years ago, when I was in my late thirties, having a wonderful friend, Tema Nason, a fellow writer, a beautiful redhead, seventy-six years old, widowed for many years, and, to her occasional exasperation and occasional delight, dating. It didn't sound much different from what I was going through. The wave of hope, the dizzying disappointment. Actually, if I remember right, I was at the beginning of a long moratorium on love. She was the one who had the juicy details to share.

"What really irritates me," she said one day, standing up with a restless surge at the memory, "is when people tell me, 'You don't look seventy-six.' What on earth am I supposed to answer? I tell them, 'This is what seventy-six looks like.' But what bugs me even more is when people talk to me as if I know what I'm doing. 'How should I know what's an appropriate response,' I tell them. 'I've never been seventy-six before.'"

I've returned to Tema's outburst again and again in my mind. "How am I supposed to know what's an appropriate response," I'll mutter in the throws of joy, passion, or despair. "I've never been thirty-seven, forty-seven, fifty-seven before." But I have a wonderful sense of Tema—of the energy and passion in her writing and her elegant, earthy and slightly imperious way of being in the world. I've always felt comforted by the vivid but reduced expectations she introduced me to. Wisdom wasn't going to shroud me anytime soon. I might even one day be seventy-six and passionately wondering, "How should I know? I've never been here before."

In the last two years, I've heard some variant of Tema's comment from a number of my trail-blazing friends, including my marvelous co-editors, and it seemed a wonderful project to compare notes far and wide. There's a lot going on after seventy, as much, or more, as there was before. If you closed your eyes and just listened to the words, it might be hard to tell the difference from thirty or fifty or sixty.

With this difference, I think. There's a lot more zest—and a lot more death. More self-acceptance. More surprise. There's a treasury of long relationships and a lot of jumping back into the roiling flow of love with both feet, ready or not. There's a lot of knowing, now that it's gone, the wonder of what we have had. There's a lot of knowing it before it goes too. And a lot of learning to love what comes to take its place when the one we love no longer knows us. It's hard to start anew, reinvent ourselves, and very few of us want to. On the other hand, life is busy engraving our skin and erasing our mental connections, stripping away our most treasured life-defining commitments. "If not now, when?" isn't a cliché, it's an imperative. But an imperative to what? "How should I know," Tema says with a snort. "I've never been here before."

The works Nancy, Megan and I chose seem to fall naturally into the categories we've used here. First off, that wonderful question, our *Overture*: How do septuagenarians make love? What is it about turning seventy that distinguishes it? What changes, what remains the same? The talk about chicks? The taste for finery? Our glee at throwing our hands up and hearing the clear crack of the whip of life?

Our second section, *View from A Distance*, gathers some of the poems and memoirs that explore what we imagine love after seventy might be like, whether we are in our thirties at the time, like Anna Steegmann, or coming close on that age ourselves, like Don Thackrey. Did we ever have a real, carnate sense of what went on between our parents? Our grandparents? When in our lives do they come back to us insisting we revision them more generously—and ourselves in the process?

The third section, *The Real Stuff*, enchants me each time I read it over. So many wonderful writers, so many distinct voices, but such a harmonic between them. We find everything here. Passion allied with something so clear-eyed and steady it stops us, shores us, helps us see anew. William Borden writes,

> and I'll be looking at you with new eyes,
> too, knowing you're hiding surprises
> in that cerebellum, and those sagging
> breasts and silver hairs are really brand
> new models, and our dandy dendrites and
> capering mitochondria are right
> now making everything a wonder.

Maureen Flannery talks of the mysterious fusion of identity that comes from long love:

> . . .
>
> It is strange that sometimes I can't feel
>
> as I touch you, which skin pads
> my fingertips and which is stretched
> across your shoulder blades
> like a suspension bridge.

Grey Held, too, talks about the relief he feels, breaking the last of the Waterford glasses from their wedding: "Actually, I'm happy/the Being Careful is over with." But not the passionate attention and presence: "I want to tuck your bangs behind your ear./ I would like to/introduce myself to you again."

Most of this section is poetry, perhaps because it best captures the bittersweet lyricism of the moment, the complexity of love over time, love until death, since death hovers like a shadow or a grace note, just like youth, everywhere you look. Ada Jill Schneider's poems play with this tension:

> . . .We watch
> our babies grow up and our parents slowly leave
> and can't take our eyes off these used-to-be
> smiling people we're converting to DVD
> so they can always live with and beyond us,
> going round and round in this once-only world.

There is anger here, loss, betrayal, and rediscovery. So many ways to know love, in so many realms, so infused that past is with this future. Sondra Zeidenstein writes, "I lie awake grieving how lost/one of us will be forever from the other, one day." Myrna Goodman plays with the letters that signify her husband's retirement:

> I spend my morning moving
> seven capital letters
> around the kitchen table.
> GOOD
> GOD
> DAMN
> DOOM
> MAD
> MAN
> GOODMAN

In the fourth section, *In Sickness and Health*, death and illness are our partners. Sylvie Terepolski muses on her friend Ketzel's question, "What about love?" and concludes, "I leave with love, death, and life all confounded in my thoughts and I know I will never sort it out. I just have to let it be."

These stories, memoirs and poems are about being as fully as possible in the presence of love and death and knowing that place to be life. Dorothy Stone writes,

> Alone, what?
> I don't choose to know.
> Don't leave.
> Don't go.

There are poignant memoirs and stories here that describe what it is to be here and losing yourself—and your loved one—at the same time. Ann Goethe captures this in "Coach":

> He said he'd forgotten the way. Almost fifty years in this
> town on this street and he couldn't find his way home.
> Talking about it, you could tell he was afraid of himself,
> his eyes cloudy and trapped looking at the same time.

So does Frank Salvidio in his poem "Shadowland":

> In this confusion, can my memory
> Of us survive if I do not survive
> In you—if you can neither hear nor see
> The common memory that keeps us alive?

In her memoir, "Waiting," Phyllis Langton describes a powerful shared consciousness between her husband George and her as they live their way into his ALS. He talks about all the ways he now waits:

> "I wait and watch myself die a little every day. It's
> probably hard for you to imagine the searing exhaustion
> I go through. I can't do anything for myself. 'Well,' you
> tell me, 'you can still breathe without difficulty. So get
> off your pity pot.'"

The same consciousness is there in the companion piece, "A Celebration of Life," heart wrenching, profoundly affirming:

> Grasping tiny fragments of your bones that made it
> through the fire and grinders, I think of the times I
> ran my hands, with tenderness and passion, over your
> muscled body. My eye are full of salt and grime. I want
> to run away, to keep your ashes with me forever.

In the fifth section, *Moving On*, we have all different levels and kinds of re-engagement, romantic and of convenience, sometimes both. There is a sense of wonder and recognition—of lost opportunity and present largesse. Mary O'Dell writes,

> When I saw you, I didn't regret the years
> I didn't know you.
> I was only glad that this is now
> and you're in it.

Anna Chance, exploring passion and detachment at seventy, writes,

> On reflection, I shall always be in a state of love. Other
> men in my life I've loved in different ways. Now, he-
> who-is-guarded won't know if I love him or not. I'm full
> of love. I love my dog, my house, my grandchildren,
> their parents, and the sun on my patio, the air, the
> bright cold New Year that brought me this new affair.

While Jack Ruszkowski, the widower in Wayne Scheer's story, observes of a woman's house he visits:

> It felt like a home, neat and clean, but a faint odor of
> yesterday's pot roast lingered. That's what he missed in
> his own home, he realized. It had been a long while
> since he smelled yesterday's dinner.

A grandmother runs off to make an impetuous marriage of convenience in Angela Conti Molgaard's "When Elsie Married Bob," and Lynn Ruth Miller, an unmarried woman nearing seventy-five, exuberantly exclaims, "I fall madly in love every day: exciting, buoyant and daring passion that overwhelms me. . . .I give away my favors freely and often because I know these romances are the kind only an old woman can enjoy." Romances that, finally, can gratefully accept the men in her life exactly as they are, just as they can accept her.

But romance, healing, full-circle, just like you find in the movies romance, can come at the most unexpected times, as Nancy Pelletier describes in "This Is Louis Wymond":

> Arriving at 80 is a shock. Where did the time go? How
> much time is left? It's neither a good nor a bad feeling—
> just one of amazement. . . . But it has a sense of ending.
> But wait!. . .Love is waiting in the wings.

In the final section, *Last Things*, our stories and memoirs are again at one remove, set for the most part in retirement homes or hospice. This is a point where people are not telling their own stories anymore—and others are opening up to take the skeletons of those lives in and cherishing them until they walk, full-fleshed and vibrant, through our imaginations. Here we hear again and again the insufficiency of language and the great gift of a re-membering presence, whether it is a grieving spouse, fellow resident in a retirement home, a friendly visitor. Who is going to hold us in imagination in our living and dying when everyone we know is gone?

In Stephanie Feuer's story of Mr. Steiner, a stroke survivor, and another retirement home resident, Margaret, we hear this question echo:

> "Did you have a lot of friends, talk about ideas and
> music and people you knew?" And then she softened.
> "Did you spend a lot of time in Paris?"
> Tears filled his eyes. His mouth contorted, the
> left side refusing to hold a shape. In more a hiss than a
> whisper, he uttered, "Yes. Oh g-g-God, yes."

Why *should* that passionate sensibility, that intensity of inner experience that resounds in everything we read here, ever stop—even when, silenced by stroke, we can't convey it? For what we realize when we finish this collection is that life after 70 is, excuse me, hot. And tender, wise, surprised, biting, grieving, kind. Something, we can tell our grandchildren, smiling wisely, slyly, shyly, they too may find.

OVERTURE

JOYCE RICHARDSON

HOW DO SEPTUAGENARIANS MAKE LOVE?

Without socks,
Without sheets,
Without counting,
Without apology.

After checking the mail,
but before supper.
After putting out the cats, but often
in front of the dogs.

After drinks,
After fights,
Afternoons,
Afterglow.

As delicate as butterflies,
As fierce as lumberjacks,
As clamorous as clowns.

With tact,
With the greatest of tact,

With no tact whatsoever.

MEET ME IN SPOLETO

If you should go first,
(as we always planned)
I being a woman,
and a little younger than you,
and I follow after...
Meet me in the Piazza Mercato...
I know you'll be waiting
under the blueblue Italian sky—lovely, but
not the only heaven we've known.

But if I should go first,
(as we've always suspected)
my being who I am, I mean
I could fall down steps
and be gone just like that.
Don't forget the Piazza Mercato
and the bar on the corner beside the face fountain...
I'll trip over the cobblestones to greet you,
to see again your blueblue eyes.
Meet me, meet me:
you, the only heaven I've known.

SEVENTY-FIFTH BIRTHDAY PARTY

"My pee is green," he says.
She looks up from cutting the chocolate cake and sneers.
Then she rolls her eyes.
"Come on, you told me to communicate," he says.
She sighs, "Tell me something I don't know."

"My pee is green," he says.
"How could you possibly know that?"

"I know you're a fucking…"

"Hypochondriac," he nods.

"And you don't have a…"

"Clue," he finishes.

She sticks out her lower lip.
"You never tell me how you feel."

"I feel very strange," he says.
"I feel upset and weird. But then…"

"Your pee is green." She tosses the words
up in the air and smiles.
She reaches for his hand.
"Do you notice, my darling, how we always
finish each other's sentences?"

"And do you notice," he adds,
"how you bake me a chocolate cake
for my birthday even though it's
your favorite and I'd rather have…"

"a present," she finishes.
She smiles. "Shut up and eat your cake."

YOU MUST TIPTOE

You must tiptoe
around a man of a certain age,
do anything to avoid an awful row.

Be even more mendacious
than you were when you were gorgeous,
only your wits will save you now.

You must dazzle
in the kitchen, kiss him in his study,
lie like you've never lied before.

"Darling, don't you remember?"
"Sweetheart, I have told you
a thousand times this month and heretofore."

"We're going to the islands;
You'll love those crazy islands,
you'll love the heat and sand and salty brine.

We'll swim among the dolphins,
sidestep all the jellyfish,
feel reckless one more time, just one more time."

You must tiptoe
when you travel, with a man of a certain age;
promise when you perform an illegal act.

You must dazzle
in the bedroom, kiss him in the ocean,
though you know for sure
he's never coming back.

JUDITHA DOWD

ALMOST OLD

This morning in the early light
as sun cut shadow into your cheek
like the bold scars of an elder tribesman,
your body curled like a comma, punctuating
                              a fallen dream.
I looked
and you were almost old,
        thin-skinned calves,
        etched balls in a cozy nest,
saw, too, my breast
                slumped against the rumpled sheet.
It was surprising
        the way the beech outside our window
has overnight shed its copper leaves,
shimmering wealth around its feet
        and every branch a newborn thing.

It's a lie that we're young only once,
        and you and I have been given our time.
But all those leaves, and your limbs bent inward,
        hunched and innocent like a child's.
I wanted to wake thee,
plight thee again in the old language,
                        my troth.

And what word tonight
      for your practiced hand
or my craving for salt,
this seagull air dense with the scent of evening?
Now in the slowness of our knowing,
      a raindrop finding its natural plain,
we've left behind the brittle verbs,
              fossils of a younger need
and faintly amusing here at the gates of our ruin.

Time,
nothing else to wait for.
But what god doesn't crave his handiwork,
listen for the *oh* of pleasure and regret,
      in even the longest season?

PATRICIA BRODIE

ROOTS

Yesterday
we saw hotels and palms distorted,
uprooted by last week's hurricane;
whitecaps to the horizon
savage waves slaying what's left of the beach.

Tonight
I hold out a wishbone after dinner
our fingers wrap around its ends
and you win

wished, you said,
as always
for your love.

BEAUTY

News Item: *The beautiful people sip champagne in the Grand Ballroom at Mar-A-Lago as they watch the opening of Fashion Week.*

We all knew she'd been a fashion model in her day.
Now eighty, she wears pink chiffon
ropes of pearls
designer scarves
to hide a frail frame
but her posture is still as elegant
as her old Powers Agency name: Summer Raynes.

Last week, at mahjong,
she told us her daughter had been
in Donald Trump's ballroom that morning
setting up the runway
bringing in the models
when he asked her to stand next to him
for a photo
and he called her the most beautiful woman in the room.

I start to watch "Project Runway" on TV,
see young designers compete—
backless evening gowns with daring necklines
tasseled party outfits....

Now I, too, want to wear tasseled silks,
bold jewelry.
Is it too late?

I ask my husband what the retired men
talk about
sitting around the heated pool.
Health, he says,
and why people move away, but mostly
they talk about 'chicks.'

TANKA

You praise my beauty
say you love my poetry
your heart beats iambs
of devotion or could that be
your testosterone patch?

EMILIE GEORGE

THE THING IS: ON TURNING SEVENTY

The thing is: to fight the momentum of amassed years rising like the claw of Hokusai's *Great Wave* above you, the hood of a poised cobra. Ride the wave, hypnotize the cobra! Hold the road against the centrifugal force of the septuagesimal S-curves pulling away from juvenescence.

The thing is: don't consider seconds as little empty cups dripping off a clock or as abacus beads sliding away from you on the time-rail, or its pendulum as a swinging scythe cutting the day into medallions of boredom upon which you whine and dine.

The thing is: to tilt Don Quixote's tilt, angle away from the ordinary. Like a sunflower gyrate toward the warmth of a Dulcinea.

The thing is: when the rime of despair grows a hoar frost on the sleeve-edge of gesture, turn inward to the spring always in season.

The thing is: if you can't go forward or retreat, swivel in place, do the divine vertigo of Dervishes, pirouette-flowers of dancers.

The thing is: to drink your existential tea and as the days line up like dominoes ready to fall in tap-dancing cadenzas, grab the tail of the surge and crack-the-whip of life!!! Hallelujah!!!

VIEW FROM A DISTANCE

DON THACKREY

SLOW TO SPEAK

Both Pa and Ma were frugal in their speech,
Communicating somehow otherwise:
A look, a touch—enough to warn or teach
A lesson with no need to verbalize.
When Pa agreed with anything he heard,
He'd pause a bit—then give one nod—slow, slight,
And only if beseeched, he'd find a word
Or two to say—distant but yet polite.
Ma's reticence, warmer—but just as still;
She went about her constant work content
To hold her counsel and complaints until
Silence became her native element.
Our folks! We wondered if a word was said
When they were young and finding love in bed.

CHRISTINA LOVIN

PHOTOGRAPH, 1975

My mother in a red coat, reclining
in the prow of a gray row boat. Gray all around.
Gray the sky. Gray the water. Gray her eyes,
although my father always called them blue.
This, in their fiftieth year together—
the children grown and gone—my father unseen
behind the camera. My mother's look coquettish
and young as any lover in this autumn shot.

Thirty years later, ten years past his death—
her health gone, four of seven children gone, gone
that bloom about her which even I, the youngest,
remember—she wastes in bed to skin and broken bone.
Your father was a keeper, she states one day
for no apparent reason. Him being only Father to me
I fail to understand. Until, when going through her things,
I pull this photo, whole, from a box of ruined prints.

ANNA STEEGMANN

HANS IN LUCK

My love for German food and the German language returned. Most Thursdays after therapy, I strolled down the three blocks of Sauerkraut Boulevard/ East 86th Street. Yorkville in the early 80s, before the onslaught of PC Richards, Victoria's Secret, and Footlocker mega stores had the flavor of a German neighborhood. Restaurants, named Heidelberg, Ideal, and Café Geiger, served *Jägerschnitzel, Sauerbraten,* and excellent draught beer. Elk's Candy carried the best marzipan this side of the Atlantic. In the evenings, zither and accordion players entertained the crowd. Before I started my long haul back to TriBeCa, I always treated myself to *Kaffee und Kuchen,* Germany's version of High Tea, at Kleine Konditorei. Their rich Black Forest tart, almost as good as my mother's, never failed to improve my mood.

In Germany, being German was an ordeal, a full time job. Every day we dealt with our parents and grandparents' guilt, the heavy load we had inherited. On American TV, my compatriots were Nazis, deranged psychiatrists, or Bavarians in Lederhosen. They were barking orders, or slapping their legs doing the *Schuhplattler* dance. I was no longer troubled or insulted by it. Here in New York, at Kleine Konditorei, I shamelessly indulged in my Germaness.

Kleine Konditorei, proud of its home cooking and *gut bürgerlich* ambiance, kept the Teutonic theme under control. No antlers on the wall, no decorative steins, or yodeling over the sound system, just immaculately clean windows and floors, red fabric chairs and sofas, starched white linen tablecloths, and fine china. New York offered a multitude of restaurant experiences, but it did not have a coffee house culture like European cities. Kleine Konditorei, a pitiable substitute for Berlin's Café Einstein was the next best thing. I could linger for hours in a comfortable upholstered chair over a *Kännchen Kaffee* without being harassed by the wait staff to place another order every twenty minutes.

Anita, the heavyset Viennese waitress, was polishing the doorknob with a table napkin as I made my way in.

"Schönen guten Tag," she chirped.

"Danke, ebenso," I answered.

Ogling the cakes and pies behind the counter, I made my way to my favorite table. From my vantage point, I could scrutinize most of the inside tables as well as the outside street action. Across from me, three old ladies with hairdos resembling corrugated sheet metal, sat with gigantic portions of tort. They spoke a strange mixture of German and English. "Der Mohnkuchen is fantastic. So lecker! Please pass mir die milk und das Sweet & Low."

I considered the special attributes of German *Kaffee und Kuchen*. Brewed with less Arabica beans, German coffee was thinner than Italian espresso, but superior to the dishwater that passed for American coffee. Americans never got torts right. Just like their saccharine smiles, their pastries were unbearably sweet. German pastries, like life, were both sweet and tart. As I sank my teeth into the scrumptious piece of *Schwarzwalder Kirschtorte*, a superb concoction of cherry sauce, flour, cream, eggs, chocolate, and Kirsch brandy, I mocked the accent I heard all around me: "Ziss Kriempuff is fäbuluss."

As I licked my spoon I thought about my therapist's question an hour ago: "Have you ever been with an older man?" and how I had rebuffed Vivian Deutsch: "No way. An older guy and me? You won't see that happen any time soon." Vivien had been adamant: "You ought to give it a try. Allow yourself to be attracted to a good kind man. A man with the qualities of a good father. It should help you move from romantic love and a fixation on sex, to sustained attachment."

Maybe she had a point. Even Freud had called romantic love "the overestimation of the romantic object."

As I surveyed the room, a man with the handsome look of an old-time matinee idol caught my eye. His Basque cap, silver unruly hair sticking out from underneath, and red scarf tied around his neck gave him a bohemian flair. He took cautious measured steps, and then rested on his cane until Anita came to his rescue. She led him to a table set for a large group of people, took his coat and helped him into his seat.

"Who is that?" I asked when she passed by.

"Hans Glück. He's a writer. Part of the Stammtisch. A group of old

Jewish folks who meet here every Thursday. They all speak German."

"You are kidding?"

"No. They've been coming here for the past thirty-five years. No one wants to wait on them. They sit forever and don't eat much. Terrible tippers."

I decided to stay and ordered a brandy. As I savored my Asbach, I eavesdropped on the discussion at their table. My ears perked up when I heard them talk about Thomas Bernhard's latest book. One man with an Austrian accent didn't like Bernhard: "How can he call Salzburg, his hometown, a terminal disease?" Hans Glück didn't like my favorite writer either. "Who does he think he is? James Joyce? Unreadable, this relentless, repetitive stuff."

How could he not like Bernhard? In my canon of western literature, next to Musil and Beckett, Bernhard was the greatest writer of our century. No one else's writing was so personal and uncompromising. Hans Glück was ignorant. How would he justify his position? I strained to listen. Against my better judgment and annoyance, I fell in love with the way he spoke. Like a bourgeois playboy in the final days of the Habsburg monarchy, his was a pure, upper class, turn-of-the-nineteenth-century German, untainted by any Anglicism. In an instant he transported me to an Arthur Schnitzler novel. Fortified by my third brandy, I asked Anita to introduce me. She did not waste time.

"Liebe Stammtischgäste, you have to meet Anna. She's from the Rhineland, but she studied in Berlin."

"Oh Berlin, my heart aches for you," Hans Glück said.

Now I had a chance to study him close-up. He had bushy, unruly eyebrows, and curious pale blue eyes. His right eye had a mind of its own and made him look almost cross-eyed. The enormous dark circles under his eyes held a lot of sorrow. But his lips were full and sensual. Somewhat melancholic. He must have been a good kisser. As if he had been able to guess my thoughts, he turned to me, took my hand and kissed it gently. "Junges Fräulein, we must get to know each other. I'm quite lonely these days. Come visit me," he pleaded. Then he rummaged through his pants pocket and produced a business card. Hans Glück, Writer, it said.

I became a regular visitor to Hans' home in Washington Heights where he had lived since the forties. His neighborhood, now populated mostly by Dominican families, had become a haven for German Jews after World War II. Other Jewish émigrés called it the Fourth Reich, but he affectionately called it Frankfurt on the Hudson. Hans had been drawn there for its close proximity to the Cloisters, "the most European of all places in New York and without a doubt the best place for a poet."

For the next year I traveled twice a month on the #1 subway from TriBeCa all the way up to the tip of Manhattan. In Hans' apartment everything was covered with dust; the furniture was tired, and the windows and curtains had not been cleaned in years. Just as I had envisioned a political émigré's home, books invaded every space. There were overstuffed bookshelves in the hallway, living room, dining room, his office, bedroom, and even in the bathroom. Piles of books rose in stacks from the floor requiring careful navigation. One careless move could send the bastions of European thought crumbling down. We had many things in common. Our love for literature. Our loathing for the horrible bread and tasteless beer in America. Coming from Berlin and accustomed to the Berliner's rough charm and sarcastic humor, we were flabbergasted by the friendliness of the American people.

"The telephone operators say 'Thank you,' 'Have a nice day' and 'You're welcome.'"

"Even the dentist called me by my first name."

Hans helped me understand the mysteries of the American psyche.

"Why do they give you their business card, act so enthusiastic, and then never call?"

"They just can't say no. They don't want to hurt your feelings."

"Why do they think I am overly critical when I'm just being honest?"

"They can't tolerate the truth. They like fantasy."

I was falling for him in a peculiar way. But when he put his hand on my knee I felt repulsed. As if I had put my fingers in an electric outlet, a shock wave reverberated through my body. Too stunned to speak, I watched him slide his hand up my leg and caress my thigh. "Are you wearing garters and stockings?" he mumbled. "I sure hope so. The invention of pantyhose was a punishment for the male species."

My shock waves turned to nausea. The idea of sex with a man his age was truly revolting. I rebutted his offer to spend the night. "You are out of your mind. I'm looking for a friend, someone to give me guidance, not orgasms." Hans, disappointed, but not defeated, insisted: "What about a man like me, aged and mellow like fine cognac? I have a lot of experience pleasing women. Anything a young man does, I can do it better."

I had no doubt. Now my experience as a Go-Go dancer came in handy. I knew how to put a man in his proper place.

"Hans, if you come on to me one more time, I'll leave and you'll never see me again."

"Schon gut, I'd rather have you as a friend than not have you at all."

Once this was settled, we kept the erotic tension at bay and for the most part got along fine. Despite our age difference, we were alike in many ways. Neither of us had found lasting happiness in love. I was married to Ernest and had started a steamy affair with Ivan. Hans had been married twice. Neither marriage lasted long. He had his reasons: "Something in me bristles at the domestication of love. The sight of the heavy oak marriage-bed repulses me. Love should be the continuation of poetry by other means." I, brought up on tragic love stories, dangerous affairs, enchanting courtesans, and women like Emma Bovary, in pursuit of their desires, was a kindred spirit. In my love for literature, I had made a mess of my life and ended up with an unbalanced mind. Maybe it was best to settle for platonic love with Hans? A former tomboy, I had always gotten along fine with men as long as I didn't turn them into my lovers. Intellectually stimulating conversations were gratifying. Maybe they'd be a good substitute for sex?

I could not have asked for a more captivating companion. Hans had known the best writers of his generation, both in Europe and the United States. They came alive in his anecdotes. The Parisian exile. Getting drunk in the Café de la Poste with Joseph Roth, one of my literary heroes. The cocktail party at John Dos Passos' house in Provincetown. Playing cricket with Langston Hughes at McDowell. Langston Hughes!

I had been to Paris too. In the Père Lachaise cemetery, I had bypassed the gravesite of Jim Morrison, the most popular destination for people my age, to pay my respects at the final resting places of Oscar Wilde and Gertrude Stein. I had been inside Freud's study in Vienna and had touched his desk and inkpot. But most of my experiences seemed second rate compared to his.

Hans, raised in a Jewish assimilated family "more German than the Germans,"amazed me with his command of the German language after more than forty years in exile. His mother tongue was the umbilical cord connecting him to his homeland. "I did not allow Hitler to destroy my love of German." He made me feel good about being German. "There's no collective guilt. Not all Germans were Nazis." When he saw that I wasn't convinced, he cleared his throat, straightened his back, and in his most dignified speech recited one of his poems.

> When I think of Germany at night
> I think of Heine,
> Novalis, Bach,
> I no longer think of Buchenwald. *

My father, the Catholic Nazi, had tried to eradicate my artistic ambitions: "No, you can't join the Drama Club. Forget about a career in the arts. Writers don't make any money, at least not during their lifetime." Hans, the Jewish Socialist, encouraged my creative desires. He came to see me play Lulu in Wedekind's "Spring Awakening." Like a proud father he clapped louder and harder than anyone else at La Mama that evening. When I showed him my poems, he complimented me: "Not bad at all. You certainly have a way with words."

We argued about literature like lovers, made up like lovers, except we weren't lovers. We had a great relationship until I lost him to another woman. He met Hannelore at an event in honor of his life's work at Goethe House where actors and actresses recited his poems and prose. At the reception Hannelore, in a tight navy blue suit, a glass of champagne in her hand, buttered him up. "I am so impressed with your work, your talent. I have read all your plays and can't decide which one is my favorite." I hated her instantly. She was a provincial school teacher in search of luster for her boring life. Maybe befriending writers would do the trick. I tried to signal Hans my disapproval. He, smitten with her big tits and long blond curls, totally ignored me.

I was thirty-two; Hannelore was fifty-seven; Hans was eighty-eight. His two-volume memoir had just been published in Germany. After a hiatus of fifty years his plays were performed again. His German publisher had invited him to a literary talk show and a book tour, but he was not able to board a plane by himself and visit his homeland. His eyesight had deteriorated to near blindness. Hannelore offered to help. When she suggested that he could live with her in Tübingen, Hans answered: "Only if you do me the honor of marrying me." She accepted. "Will you help me shop for a wedding suit? " he asked me. "She won't let me wear my old tuxedo, the one I bought for my second marriage. She thinks it's bad luck."

The Nice Guys Livery Cab service took us downtown. As we rode along the Westside Highway, Hans swayed along to the Spanish music on the radio. I felt attacked by the romantic words: There was no *amor, vida preciosa*, no *futuro* and no *afección* for me. The spectacular views of the Hudson River left me cold. Hans clearly enjoyed himself. "Should I go for a black or navy suit?" he asked. I shrugged my shoulders. I didn't care what kind of suit he got.

"Don't you think black is too funeral? I want an upbeat suit, one that shouts optimism and joy."

"Let's go for navy then," I said, trying not to sound weepy.

"What a marvelous day, made for poetry," he raved, puffed his chest and started to recite:

> Wie soll ich meine Seele halten, daß
> Sie nicht an deine rührt? Wie soll ich sie
> Hinheben über dich zu anderen Dingen?**

"Don't you love Rilke?"

I used to, but now I hated him. I was glad when we finally reached Trinity Place. Syms, housed in an ugly utilitarian building, boasted to hold the largest selection of off-price clothing in America. We made our way to the men's department where hundreds, maybe thousands of suits were awaiting adoption. "I'll sit down. You go and pick the right one for me. I'm a 40 Regular, the same size as when I arrived in New York in 1944," Hans said with pride.

I roamed the canons of male formal attire, the rows of suits with orange, blue, green and yellow tickets and finally found his size. Mad at Hannelore for taking Hans away from me, for not letting him wear his old tuxedo, the one that could have bestowed bad luck on his third marriage, I searched the racks for the ugliest suit. Why should Hans look handsome for her? Then a pang of guilt struck me. Who was I to jinx this marriage? Hans deserved to be happy. I picked out three elegant, distinguished looking suits and brought them over. A salesclerk nodded his approval, took them from me and guided Hans behind the black curtain to the dressing rooms. I sat down and studied the signs for on-site tailoring. The place was depressing. Hans, in his socks and chic Calvin Klein suit, was helped by the salesclerk to the platform covered with sad red threadbare carpeting. I watched the measuring tape swing from the salesclerk's neck. Hans moved as close as possible to the mirror, then turned around and scrutinized himself from every angle.

"Don't I look elegant," he exclaimed. "I swear this suit takes years off my life. I feel sixty again."

"Your father looks marvelous," the salesclerk said. "I hear the wedding is in two days." He knelt down, took a pin out of his mouth and started to cuff Hans' pants. "You are lucky that we do rush tailoring."

I didn't feel lucky. In fact, I tried hard not to grind my teeth. When Hans came back out in his old clothes, he sat down next to me. We would have to wait to have the pants hemmed and the suspender buttons sewed on. Hans turned to me. Even with one blind eye, he could tell I was upset.

"What's the matter, Anna? Aren't you happy for me?"

"I'm happy for you, but I'll miss you." I tried hard not to choke.

"You can always visit us."

"That's not the same."

"There are telephones."

"I know. But I'll miss our *Kaffeeklatsch*. Your stories."

"Look, this is my last chance to feel young again, to be celebrated for my talent. After all the wrong women, I have to take a chance at love." Hans lifted up my chin. "You're not crying, are you? Don't be sad. You'll find the right one too, I know."

I swallowed hard. Why would I want anybody else?

I had attended plenty of green card weddings, including my own. Elegant affairs staged in downtown lofts, East Village rooftops, or trendy Japanese restaurants. Gay American artists hoping for an easier life in Berlin or Hamburg married Germans with expired tourist visas. Hans and Hannelore's wedding, however, was the real thing.

Getting off the elevator on the ninth floor, I was shocked to find crates of books stacked up in the hallway. Was Hans moving out? Inside his apartment the piles of books were gone, the chairs and tables were freed of them too. My nose led me right to the living room. His desk and dining table had been pushed together to create an enormous buffet, weighed down with his friends' contributions to his potluck-wedding feast. Leo Blumenthal had brought his famous *Würstelgoulash*, Elfriede Goldberg her chicken paprika and Nicole Edelmann her *Buletten*. There were *Lachsbrötchen, Rouladen,* and even my childhood's beloved *Heringsstip,* the dish I had eaten on my first outing to a restaurant with my father. I unwrapped my contribution to the party and squeezed two loaves of Zabar's apricot strudel, Hans's favorite, into the tiny space left on the table. I thought about all the times in my life when food had been my solace. A great meal had often provided a much superior experience than most sex, so often mediocre and disappointing. I feasted my eyes on the Central European delicacies in front of me. I had not seen such quantities of scrumptious foods since my First Communion. Why wasn't I tempted? Why had I lost my appetite? I consoled myself with Henkel sparkling wine.

Leo Blumenthal, who fled Vienna in 1938, sat down at the piano. The guests decked out in thirty-year-old tuxedos and faded cocktail dresses were giddy with excitement. When Leo started the first beats of *Zwei Herzen im Dreivierteltakt,* Hans walked with careful measured steps toward his bride, bowed, took her hand, kissed it, and then pulled her close. He looked like a young man escorting his sweetheart to the debutante ball. They danced an elegant waltz. Some of the wedding guests formed a circle around them and sang along the schmaltzy tune.

> *Ein Viertel Frühling und ein Viertel Wein,*
> *Ein Viertel Liebe, verliebt muß man sein.*
> *Zwei Herzen im Dreivierteltakt,*
> *Wer braucht mehr, um glücklich zu sein?****

When they stopped thunderous cheering and clapping erupted. Hans, overcome with emotion, took a handkerchief from his pocket, wiped the sweat from his forehead, cleared his throat and addressed his guests: "*Liebe Freunde* thank you for helping me celebrate the happiest day of my life." Dapper in his navy suit, pink tie and rose pinned to his lapel, he looked like a professor emeritus, a distinguished scholar of philosophy. Hannelore had even trimmed his nose hairs for the occasion.

"Earlier this morning we were at City Hall. The most marvelous place in all of New York City. Every single person in the room was filled with hope. I'm so glad you came to send us off. Hannelore and I will be leaving for our honeymoon on Wednesday. I won't be coming back to Washington Heights or New York City."

"Let's have a toast to the *Brautpaar,*" Leo said.

Everyone chimed in. *Hoch solln sie leben.* Bride and groom blushed to a thunderous applause.

    Leo Blumenthal sat down again and started to play a slow, melancholy tango. Mrs. Goldberg, in long black gloves and a too tight bottle green satin dress that revealed a lot of wrinkled cleavage, positioned herself in dramatic fashion next to the piano and started to sing

> *We sat*
> *in der kleinen Konditorei,*
> *had coffee and cake.*
> *No need to say a single word,*
> *I understood you right away.*

It felt as if a soccer ball struck my stomach. This was our song. Die kleine Konditorei, I had met Hans there. Mrs. Orenstein, a holocaust survivor, who had lost her husband to cancer three month ago, turned to me and said: "Isn't it marvelous to find love at his age?" Trim and petite, she nibbled on her strudel. I stared at her thinning bluish hair, at a loss for words. A lady in a crimson suit came to my rescue, pulling Mrs. Orenstein to the dance floor. It was my chance to run off. At the buffet, I quickly downed two glasses of champagne. I had to get away from the radiant *Brautpaar,* the happy guests, the joyous laughter.

    Careful to avoid anyone who might engage me in a conversation, I made my way to the back of the apartment. Between the coat rack and the bathroom, I sat down on the floor and gave myself over to a brooding unhappiness. How did people fall in love and stay in love? They had to be born with that knowledge that eluded me all my life. I wondered if I'd ever find lasting love and grow old with a man. Someone who'd walk a mile to get me hearty black bread for breakfast and remembered that plum butter was my favorite spread. I sat for hours, and only snuck out to fill up my glass. I felt like a suitcase abandoned at the airport's conveyor belt. Full of treasures, but unwanted and forgotten. *Bestellt und nicht abgeholt.* No one to retrieve me.

---

*Hans Sahl: Denk ich an Deutschland in der Nacht
**How shall I hold on to my soul, so that
It does not touch yours? How shall I lift
It gently up over you to other things? Rainer Maria Rilke, *Lovesong*
***Robert Stolz

JULIE PREIS

MESSAGING MY FATHER

Since you've been deaf, I speak to you straight on,
holding your eye until you answer me
or tire of trying. The less you speak,
the more I chatter. You accept it all
as praise whether you hear or not. How long
before talk fails entirely? Just in case,

I've saved your words like treasure: on the phone
before your bypass. Your fury when you learned,
at sixty-three, your brother did not have
the same mother as you. The rare surprise
of your letter after I left home. I want to hold
that letter now, to make you understand

how I have hoarded these stored coins
imprinted with your likeness, with your voice.

KEEPSAKE

In my mother's house was a box
with my name on it:
diplomas, cards, mementoes
forgotten or ignored.
Hospital baby bracelet,
white circlet of beads
the size of milk teeth.

On birthday eighty-four
she faces me, the box
held formally between us.
Suddenly she pivots,
thrusts it at my daughter
aiming her words at me:
You'd only throw this in the trash.
I feel an unaccustomed power
as the parcel changes hands.

In six months my father's dead
and my mother can't stop
giving me things: the poems
he read to us at night
(I'm Nobody! Who are you?
Are you—Nobody—Too?);
my grandmother's silk dress;
favorite childhood novels
yellowed with age.

Before she clears the house
I wander the rooms
hunting for relics.
In my high school yearbook
my photo has been scissored out.
I remember doing that.

Now I visit her and bring a box
of stories with her name on it.
I pick through the contents
holding odd fragments to the light.
Tell me about this one, I say.
We sit that way for hours.

OCEAN CITY, MD

He knew just when
to duck a wave
and when to go
with it. She'd keep
watch from her chair,
cloth hat pulled down
against the sun.
On a calm day
she'd wade shin-deep
in rolled-up pedal pushers.

Into his eighties
he body-surfed
until the traitor
nerves deadened his
feet to the sand.
Now that he's gone
she speaks of sex,
the easy way
he lived inside
his skin, the way
his face would suddenly pop

through the cresting
wave that bore him
back to shore where
he'd land, smile and
hitch up his trunks.
No need to shout
or whistle. Each
knew the other
saw; for both, this
was their pleasure.

CARL PALMER

HER CANDLE

I've got so many candles that I've never burned...
a marriage candle,
a first communion candle from one of the kids,
a bicentennial candle,
a millennium candle.
So many candles that I've never burned.

However, her candle I've burned for over twenty years,
not every day, but most everyday.
A memory of what once was,
of what we'd had,
we, me and her.
Her candle,
originally voluptuously large,
beautifully ornate,
burning bright, hot and fast.
We were young then.

Gradually her candle became hollow
with most of the outside still holding fast.
Dusty with age.
The wick long lost.
Hollowness temporarily filled with a tealight candle.
Certain songs, movies or moods
seem to rekindle the freshness,
remind me of when her candle was new.

In the light of day, reality blazes.
Her candle actually a hollow shell,
so hard to visualize as it once was,
as in last night's memory.
Beginning to wonder,

continuing to wonder,
if after all this time,
I shouldn't just throw it out.
This foolish vigil.
This senseless old man.
End this memorial, this ritual and move on.

But, as the room again grows dark,
the many candles that I've never burned,
remain so....
A new tea candle
and she is back.
We, me and her.
Her candle.
And ... my thoughts
of twenty years ago.

SERENITY

not remembering
the nice man's name
in her wedding picture

SENIOR MOMENT

I just had a senior moment.
I didn't forget something,
I remembered something.
I just remembered how my mom
would see or hear something
reminding her of something I did
when I was small, getting that smile
in her eyes, looking back and
seeing me in my cowboy hat.
"Stick'em up Mommy."
I remember her senior moment,
as she explained it,
not forgetting, but remembering.

Now I have them, a visit back,
a reminder, like it was yesterday.
My senior moment just happened
as I watch the young mother
herd her 6 children, 3 boys and 3 girls
across the street to the old brick church.
She checks each one before entering,
stops short, kneels down
in front of the oldest boy,
turns his head side to side,
holds his chin, takes a tissue
from her purse, licks it and
rubs the smudge from his cheek.

HER NEW ROOM

The house was small
where she raised her five children,
but not as small as her new room.

She lived in her house fifty-two years,
but only for a couple of months now
in her new room.

She loomed large in her small house,
yet now seems so tiny
in the corner of her new room.

Her house held the aroma of flower sachet
with smells of delicious wonderment
flowing warmly from her kitchen.

Her new room has the reek of medicine
with an underlying odor
of pine oil disinfectant.

She seemed to know everyone
wherever she went
and everyone knew her.

Today she needed to be reminded
of her daughter's name
as Judy sat there holding her mother's hand.

Waiting in her new room
she asks once more
if it's time to go back home.

JOAN DOBBIE

LOVE POEM
with my grandparents in mind

We were building a pond together:
Bring those stones, you said, here hold this plastic.
And as I carried, and pulled, lifted, and lay down,
and you carried and pulled, lifted, and lay down,

I felt as if we'd been together, you and I,
for so many years, there'd never been a time
without the two of us
                        and never would be.

As we sat in our lawn chairs, lightly touching fingers,
watching our fountain rise up and rain down
over our statues and stones and
water, keeping our pond alive,
I remembered my grandparents, already in their 80s,

how they'd sat on their back yard bench, almost shyly
holding hands, looking out over their garden
that they grew together again & again every summer
of my childhood

content with their five or six
healthy corn stalks, and their tiny, burgeoning
tomato patch, almost blushing if we children
should happen to notice
how they nourished one another, that for them

after Kristalnacht, shipwreck, loss of family,
livelihood, language—
every badge of self-respect, they still had one another, and
this small garden was enough.

ALTON BAKER PARK
Summer 2005

He has Alzheimer's.
She has dementia.

He unbuckles his pants
instead of the seatbelt.

She dials the remote
instead of the phone.

He loses his language.
She can't hold her pee.

He was, once, at least locally,
famous & powerful:

loved, truly loved.
Sometimes hated.

She was, at least in her family,
unstoppable.

Now they are who they are,
simple as that.

(It wasn't so long back, really,
that they met one another

& we were all saying, "How cute.")
Now he's forgetting her name

& she's forgetting to care
all that much.

Don't feel superior.
Let go of your pity.

See how they sit,
(when you place them)

side by side on the bench
holding hands?

See how they smile at the
clouds drifting by?

May we all, in our dotage,
be so lucky.

J. J. STEINFELD

IT IS YOUR NINETIETH SUMMER, YOU TELL ME

We reach for the same poetry book
by a young hotshot poet
with an old man's eye for sorrow.
I hand you the thin volume
as if I had attempted a theft
and recoiled with remorse.
It is your ninetieth summer
you tell me, and I am as tall as your husband
who you describe with soft resignation:
a solemn, untidy, unruly man
who died climbing a mountain
of wine and whiskey bottles
during your sixty-eighth summer.
I do not count my summers
I whisper among the book browsers
but I do look over my shoulder
and see my distant youth weeping—
inarticulate grievance, I admit,
but grievance all the same.
You remember the first time you made love
but sometimes you forget your address.
I smile uneasily, straining to recall my first time
knowing my address all too well.
I have forgotten so much
you say, looking at the book's back cover,
and fingers trembling,
touch the young poet's photo
read with difficulty, lips quivering,
about the keen eye for humanity's foibles and fears.

What will I forget? I inquire,
of the woman and of the god of memory—
the god of memory, I repeat,
an entreaty, perhaps a sad reflex.
God has taken most of your memory,
you lament, your eyes seeming to be remembering,
and you ask me to take your arm
and sing with you
the song that made you believe in love
and never getting old
the words to which
you remember as clearly
as during your nineteenth summer
when, you say, love exceeded history.

ROXANNE HOFFMAN

THE DATING SCENE AT 80

Yes, there is a dating scene at 80! *Just who did you think was buying all that Viagra?*

My mother is a widow in her 80's. She's 83, I think. And being 83 she's starting to forget stuff like her glasses, her teeth, her walker, *her age.* Some things she never forgets:

- Her lipstick, Revlon's fire engine red *Forever Scarlet.*
- Her pick up line—"My middle name is *Flora Selva.* It means Flower of the Jungle."
- And her black *stiletto* pumps! (Just why did you think she *needs* the walker?)

The other day, we're in Central Park and my mother strikes up a conversation with a lime-green parrot perched on this guy's shoulder. Apparently, she and the parrot are both from Ecuador. (The parrot speaks excellent Spanish. And Mom, she's pretty good at Parrot.) And the guy, it seems he's a collector. He collects exotic creatures:

- Parrots,
- Iguanas,
- Lava Lizards,
- Chinchillas,
- Spider Monkeys,
- Blue Morpho Butterflies,
- Ocelots,
- Pythons,
- And *Women…*

They exchange phone numbers and negotiate a rendezvous at the Cowgirl bar in the West Village. (I'm talking about Mom and the owner of the parrot, not the parrot, here. Of course, the parrot was pretty cute.)

After we get home I rib my mom about her date: "You're picking them a bit young. That guy could not have been a day over 55."

Mom says:

> "So? I'm 69. Okay, okay! Give or take a couple of years. Who's counting? Look when you get older you'll understand.
>
> Let me tell you about the dating scene at 80:
> - There's the dead.
> - There's the living dead.
> - Then there are the 80-year old body-builders with 18-year old girlfriends.
>
> This pretty much leaves 50-something guys that don't want to commit."

Yesterday, we're dining at her favorite burger joint and this good-looking guy asks Mom to pass the ketchup. Mom passes me a napkin with a note on it:

> "We're sisters. I'm 50, you're 35. And just remember: You were an accident."

Needless to say, within moments, she had lined up a date for Saturday night. On the way out, she leans over to me and says:

> "Now you know why this is my favorite burger joint!"

Mom has gotten so good at picking up men that my single girlfriends hang out with her to pick over the leftovers! She told me the secret to her success:

> "At my age I have less hang-ups than when I was younger. At 69, you don't have to worry about long-term commitments. An hour or two is a long-term commitment.
>
> *Just churn them and burn them.*

As far as selecting men:

- Breathing is good.
- A pulse is good.
- Ambulatory is better.

And I don't get bored. Everything is always new."

"Everything is always new? Mom, at your age haven't you heard and seen everything?"

"One of the great thing about being 69 is I forget everything that was just said. *(A short pause.)* By the way, what were we just talking about and who are you?"

Mom has apparently been having memory lapses for quite some time now. It seems she forgot how old she was when she was dating my dad in the 50's. She told my father she born in 1931 when really she was born in 1921! Her reason: "Men die young!"

Here's my advice:

- To you married ladies: Take care of your man. Don't rack up the charge cards to the max. Don't nag him to take out the garbage. In fact, take out the garbage yourself. And start shoveling the snow.
- To you guys: Remember guys, there's the dead, the living dead and 80-year old body builders with 18-year old girl friends. It's your future. I'd hit the treadmill now.
- Single ladies: My mother is checking out the Metropolitan Museum of Art on Sunday. Meet her in the lobby of the Museum at 1PM. You're guaranteed a date for Saturday night!

THE REAL STUFF

WILLIAM BORDEN

EVERYTHING NEW

I read that every two years the brain
reorganizes itself—neurons shoot out,
ganglia gang up, axons agitate, neuro-
transmitters split everywhichway—
and that every year or so (my memory's
chancy) the entire body renews itself—
new blood, novel bones, fresh fat, modish
muscles, pristine proteins—the works!

Even though I look familiar in the mirror
and to my friends—never mind "Putting
on weight?" and "What happened to your hair?"
—I am new as next year's calendar.
I'm talking complete overhaul,
all-out revolution inside and out.

My brain is making new neuronal
pathways just thinking about this.

I'm not even going into
Heisenberg and his Uncertainty
or Gödel's monkey wrench into the gears of logic.
I'm not mentioning Buddhism's bouncy ballads
to impermanence, recycling souls, esoteric renewals. I

just want you to know, when
you see me tomorrow, you
might think you recognize
the same old Bill, but you'll
be looking at a new model,

even if the parts, after all
these years of replenishment,
are coming out faulty—skin flaps,
gray beard, age spots, limp, aches—

and I'll be looking at you with new eyes,
too, knowing you're hiding surprises
in that cerebellum, and those sagging
breasts and silver hairs are really brand
new models, and our dandy dendrites and
capering mitochondria are right
now making everything a wonder.

LETTER

That letter you sent
in which you told me
you would love me forever
did not arrive.

That was years ago.
I blame the post office,
not you. Should I still
wait?

We've married other people.
We have children, grandchildren.
Should I wait anyway?
A stamp costs more now.

I don't look for a letter
every day. I'm not nuts.
Only sometimes, when I open the mailbox
at the end of the drive
(my magazines have been forwarded promptly,
and the bills, of course)
and there's a strange envelope,
my name handwritten
in a possibly familiar script,
my heart jumps
just a little, and I slip the envelope
into my pocket, to open
later when I'm alone,
but I'm asked only for money,
not love, to help
the handicapped
or the students in an Indian school.

I keep the key chains, the embossed pencils,
the tiny license plates, reminders
of the sweetness of a lipstick,
the scent of Soft Shoulders, the rustling of leaves
in the wind on a summer afternoon,
Jo Stafford singing "You Belong to Me."

CREAMY LOVE PASTA

one cup chopped onion
kiss cook's tears
sauté

olive oil aroma
filled Madrid
years ago

peel garlic
lots
chop

your wild
scent
my fingers

sauté
garlic
briefly

lovely things
burn quickly

chop tomato
juicy
desire

sprinkle flour
make paste
thick
as solitude
when
you're gone

dump
tomato's
insouciance

simmer
afternoon's
longing

add cream
—to hell with doctors!—

bubble
carefully
ardor's
bosomy
simmer

sprinkle feta
parmesan
pepper

pinch
oregano
your breath

spaghetti ready?

mix—twirl—swirl

Creamy Love Pasta

in a blue
hand-thrown
bowl

glass of wine
dark red
as old desire
young lust

eat
in
bed

RECKLESS LOVE
—For Nancy

Oh, those tears from onions
greeting me at the door,
the faded muumuu from Hawaii,
pork chops with pineapple—
the walk later that night
in North Beach holding hands,
Irish coffee at the Buena Vista—
you engaged to someone else—
should I kiss you anyway?

Forty-eight years, three children,
seven grandchildren later,
I'd say it was the onions,
that gustatory precognitive weeping
for what we might have missed
that knocked me sideways
into certain reckless love.

THE SNIPE'S DEATH-DEFYING FALL OF LOVE
—For Nancy

This morning when I went out walking
I heard the frantic whirr of sky
flying through the snipe's wings
as he dove headlong toward the earth,
lovesick and open-hearted, to win
the love, or at least the notice,
of the coyly listening, demurely hiding,
lady snipe.

       Now, tonight, as we climb
into bed, you can hear the wind
whistle past my feathers, hear
the wild buzz of my heart, lost
to fate and gravity, as I hurtle
madly, recklessly through the years
falling always whizzingly
for you.

MAUREEN TOLMAN FLANNERY

SUPPLY MAN

My sweet, unchecked king of wretched excess,
bringer home of the bacon
(and a dressed-out side of beef
plus a couple bushels of tomatoes
from the roadside stand on the
way home from the locker plant,)
my lucky winner of bread—
and cake and foodstuffs in such quantities
as to feed the hungry in several drought-struck countries,
my treater to more that we need or can eat,
my consumer, my grower, my carrier home,
my willing getter of what we're out of—
plus ten extra bags full for *just in case*,
my hero of the farmers' market,
placer of case lots on the pantry floor,
banned from Sam's club for lack of judgment,
my believer that more is more than less
and too much is, more or less,
more than enough,
but what's really best is wretched excess.

Who do you expect to be feeding,
our grandchildren having all dispersed?
There are only the two of us here.
Come, my lean huntsman,
my truckload truck-farmer,
buyer of stuff and thrower of parties,
put aside your "putting up."
Set u-pick-em blueberries on kitchen chairs.
Let the three ripe melons get soft on the sill,

and peaches go soggy under gray fuzz.
Leave sweet corn unshucked in a pile.
Come to me with your excess.
Till the first of us consumes the last day,
I will make space
for all the abundance you bring to me.
Let's make hay, make room,
make sure we don't run out.

ASPECT OF AGING

Through macular degeneration,
I stare into your strong, familiar features.
How kind is your skin's slow slackening
that it lets me see my own chronology,
gentle, if muddled as the first words of our grandson.

We can be each other's mirror
in the faithfulness of honest aging,
not to recoil from smile lines
creased into our present presentation
as the folds of an old love note.

My own growing old is put at ease
by the truthful loosening of your face
and dark places where the sun
has shone ambiguous rays
upon youthful days of field work
and vigorous play.

In each other's gaze
we learn to claim a countenance we've earned
like a paycheck for a job well done.

Watching a man's aspect
grow more handsome,
being framed in gray,
I think we may go graciously
to that place of knowing
past all recall of pertinent matters
to a way of being
in which nothing matters but love.

IDENTITY

Every night, as we surrender bodies to the bed,
air from deep inside your chest,
that blew a warm wind across your heart,
bathes itself in ivy on the window sill

and travels through my lungs to bring
the rhythms pulsing in your heart to mine.
Seven times since we have been together
our whole bodies have exchanged,

dissolved completely and rebuilt themselves
out of particles of each other's skin
rubbed off on our sheets and towels,
of food that grows behind the house where

we buried the placentas of our children,
of the air that forms a lemniscate
between our arching diaphragms.
Your substance has made hermitage

in the darkest caves of my country.
My fluids have dried like stucco
around the support timber of your house.
Is it strange that sometimes I cannot feel,

as I touch you, which skin pads
my finger tips and which is stretched
across your shoulder blades
like a suspension bridge.

THE LAST TIME

Old lovers, their bodies slack, blue veined,
with scaly brown patches emerging on skin
the way backs of turtles rise out of ponds,
respond predictably, tenacious in the way
they cling as they carry one another on
to the next time.

Faster than the last thing she just said,
he can pull to mind the flow of the skirt
she was wearing when he first saw her
coming out of that other church.
And some nights he needs to rest in nothing more
than the warmth of her familiar skin against his chest.

In reverie she can feel his urgent
stubbled cheek against her neck
on the nights he leaned her young hips
against the corn crib and pleaded.

Alternating health and weakness,
they love more deeply as pulsing is less intense.
Sensing a conclusion, they might be inclined
to sanctify one last conjugal act—

create a potent memory where recent happenings elude;
or perhaps, one afternoon,
having attacked their passion with a vengeance,
decide, *this is too damn much work,*
and simply give it up.

But tonight she just curls up into his sleeping S,
is lulled by the noise of his night breathing,
cradles his soft member in her cupped hand
and supposes that the last time was
the last time.

FIT

the rising cuneiform bones of her feet
press against the arches of his soles
his heels nestle into her ankles
the ridges of her shins jut
into the muscles of his calves
her knee caps against the angle
behind his bent knees
the front of her thighs on the back of his
his round buttocks resting
like twin babies into the cradle of her pelvis
her abdomen curved around his backside
her arm across his side
in the indentation of his waist
her hand cupped over his scrotum
like a chapel dome

behind the gentle rhythm of his vitality
her face pressed to his shoulder blades
whispering feathers
forming
of soft words
his wings

GREY HELD

THINGS BREAKING IN THE HOUSE

First, the false promise
of shatterproof crockery.
Then the table lamp
tumbled into darkness.
Then from the top shelf
of the linen closet
the steam iron fell
onto my head, knocking
the tears out. Tonight
a wine glass trembles
as if by whim. Then
that etched Waterford
wedding gift falls and
splinters. She asks me
if I'm angry that
the only survivor
from the set of six is
now, too, broken.
Actually, I'm happy
the Being Careful is over with.

STATISTIC

Half the marriages break up
before the thirteenth year. Gone:
the calypso that once played.
Gone: the grace of the marimbas,
the steel drums in the straight-away.
On our honeymoon, what did we know
of the perpetual trellis that raising
children is, the consistent drench
of monthly bills, life
insurance, memberships, and the requisite
home repairs, a better screw gun,
the better tub of gunk
to strip the buildup in the space
between oven and vent. It has
taken me twenty years to discover
cracks in my apparent happiness,
my own capacity for cowardice,
all my petty exits. Still
I am amazed when she sets the table
with our wedding silver,
fills the centerpiece with mangos,
kumquats, kiwis that open like geodes,
papayas and Medjool
dates, lustful and clustered,
and I am happy again
just to watch her breathe
just to watch her
knit. The clicking needles turn
some boundless timeline
into thousands of closures

and openings, so that marriage may
put on its sweater,
go out into the world—
no weeping unwept
nor any laughter unlaughed,
though of course there are
roadblocks and holdbacks,
so many pitfalls—
and it will return, for we are
lock and lock bolt, cup
and saucer. Everything completed.

LOVE

When no prophet sings
at night from out of my sleep,
when no bus stops here,
when the clouds are
bruised and breakable,
and true and false mottle in my heart,
when the day's parade has frayed
me. Even if I'm vexed
and restless and go in
a direction west of flattery.
Even when I'm drooped
in my own confusion,
and storm out the door
to walk the flagstones,
she'll open that door,
she'll follow. She'll talk
and I'll answer, as best I can,
even if I'm too tired
to dress in a suit of words.

ANOTHER MORNING

Look at my wife's sleeping hands,
blue vessels showing.
Look at her lifeline—
I think how perfectly last night
her fingers ran
like rainwater over the ridges
of my ribs and down
my spine. She rouses.
What's the matter? she asks,
when she catches me watching.
Low numbness creeps from my feet
to my groin, where that slackening pillar,
that monument, tilts, skids
down the slope of my thigh,
stone by stone. I turn back
my half of the patchwork,
get up, put on a T-shirt,
tiptoe down each wooden tread,
each riser like a reason I should
cry. Instead I do laundry,
divorcing the darks from the lights,
untying the knotted drawstring
on the sweatpants. I'm bored
with gradual mismanagement,
with every discrepancy
between what I remember
and what is correct.

ANNIVERSARY

After lunch on the beach we shake
out the blanket,
making the tension let go.
Our eyes meet. I pick up
our crumpled sandwich bags, the empty
soda cans, your beaded sandals.
Those hermit crabs are fighting
over that quahog. The tide is
coming. Come on.
Let's sip Cabernet on the balcony,
let's go dancing,
brave that parquet. I promise
I'll be different from how I've been
shying away. Will you let me
undo the buttons of your blouse,
let me feel your
breasts compress against my chest?
I want to tuck your bangs behind your ear.
I would like to
introduce myself to you again.

ADA JILL SCHNEIDER

ROMANCE

To think such passion can come
with one click on your remote control.
Shostakovich's violin solo,
Romance, plays over and over,
as long as we wish, till we're rhapsodic.
I love how we click, the way
we push away the years, fluff them
out above our king-sized bed,
then cover ourselves in their warmth.

Our son once said if it weren't for sex,
he'd be gay—women are trouble.
What he meant was *love* is trouble.
The give and take, how the route
to rapture so quickly turns into a rut—
the phonograph needle scratching
annoyance and anger deep into
the same old groove. But haven't we stuck
it out from vinyl through tape to CD's?

Old love may be expensive, but it's worth
every argument, every bouquet of apology.
Not gaudy gift-wrap or French ribbon.
I mean fine-tuning, upgrading *our* music.
Click on Shostakovich again, Love,
and acting from within (where I'm sixteen)
I'll take your crinkled loving face
into my two age-spotted hands
and kiss you like there's no tomorrow.

SPLICING PORNO FILMS

He can't take his eyes off the young me
on the screen. My alluring smile, slim hips,
perky breasts that beckon him again and again:
at our wedding, a trip to Cuba, in my classroom,
in a two-piece bathing suit holding the baby.
His heart pumps fast. Everything in him rises,
overwhelmed. He wants me right now.
Right now, he reaches out
and massages my seventy-year-old shoulders
because he knows what I like.
I tease and talk to him in ways he wants
because I, too, know. I know.
And I wonder if he is touching the young me.
Yes. Oh, yes.
What a winning combination that would be.
Yesterday's body with today's expertise.

REEL TIME

The slim, old us on eight millimeter film—
see how we moved with purpose and plans:
first baby steps, family trips, new bikes,
baseball games, chocolate birthday cakes
in the shape of eights. The old us can't begin
to imagine how fifty years can pass. But we can
as we sit here splicing our life together, rolling time
back and forward, aware of oncoming change.
I know these little kids swimming in the pool
so well, I could, even now, step in
with fudge brownies and stop their bickering.

But I don't really know the old us I see rushing
through these reels. Not inside out, like I know
the new us with our little show called *Mortality*.
We scan frame after frame of Passover Seders,
Thanksgiving dinners, anniversaries,
proms and ice-hockey games. We watch
our babies grow up and our parents slowly leave
and can't take our eyes off these used-to-be
smiling people we're converting to DVD
so they can always live with and beyond us,
going round and round in this once-only world.

WAITING FOR YOU

Your plane isn't due till six-nineteen.
It's only two o'clock but I'm prepared,
hair washed, legs shaved, make-up on,
jumping and clean as a Lubavitcher
fresh from the *mikvah*.
How could it be that I want you,
want you so much after all these years!

Remember Fort Benning, Georgia?
Me holed up reading all week
at the Shady Pines Motel,
washing my hair, doing my nails,
waiting and waiting. Then
two sweet hours together
at Friday night service with sandwiches.
Weekend leave, you in fatigues
and combat boots, walking backwards,
waving goodbye across the field,
falling into a ditch,
coming up smiling.

When you come home each evening,
I feel I've come home too.
Our parents fled from the same
little town in Poland. We would've
been slaughtered if we lived there.
One day the *chevra kadisha*
will cleanse my dead body,
wash my hair, wrap me in a clean
white shroud of seven layers,
preparing me to meet God.
But, heresy of all heresies, my love,
I will be preparing to meet you.

RUTH SILIN

BEACH SCENE

They shared a beach towel,
his hand on her thigh, her fingers
on his shoulder, their faces
turned to the sun.
His torso was tanned, his muscles bulged,
the logo on his gym bag boasted Gold's Gym.
Her bright blue bikini barely covered
her smooth bronzed skin, taut midriff,
exposed cleavage, her layered blond hair
ruffled from the sea breeze, blew across his face.

We sat near them under an umbrella,
our paperbacks still inside the Delta tote bags,
souvenirs from the years that the airlines
gave them out free.
I looked at muscle man.
He looked at gold goddess.
My partner's wisps of gray hair were hidden
by his Cape Cod cap, his puffy paunch
the kind you see in diet ads, my sagging body
partially concealed by a beach cover-up, my hair
in need of help from Clairol, our pale skin
pathetically exposed.
We looked at each other, reached for our books
and smiled.

RULES OF LOVE

When I was young and very wise I knew
That love was mine to own and waste,
like air and laughter,
an endless supply
When I was young and very wise my blood flowed fast,
I walked deliberate and provocative.
I knew the exact amount of smile to
make him mine.

When I grew old and not so wise
I forgot the way to purse my lips and tilt my head and maybe
Hum a tune like "Fly Me To The Moon" or
"I'll Be Seeing You."
I forgot the scent of tweed and after-shave and
The sweet smell of a man's sweat.
I forgot how to iron a shirt and make
A decent steak.

How quickly it came back.
A hand on my shoulder, the opening of a door,
A valentine.

My heart forgot that it was old.
My feet remembered to keep rhythm with the music.
And in the end
I rediscovered love.

PAUL SOHAR

PASSING THE SEVENTY-MILE MARK

the car wheels are squealing,
too many sneaky curves,
too many blinding headlights and
signs that still come as a surprise,

yet the landscape can fake
the familiar, the way its hips
befriend the sun and
the lookout points slide under the car;

perhaps the trip is already over,
and I keep going around in circles,
the hereafter comes to me
only as a valley filled with fog.

But then why the tire squeals,
why this jumper cable around my neck?
Why this empty paper cup if it's
too heavy even when I'm sitting down?

A youthful voice from other trips might call
out to me through the fog now and then.
I'm looking hard at a map but it stays
blank, devoid of place names, rivers, roads,

but suddenly I hear a voice from behind
the blank stare, a voice so full of
distant vistas and beautiful sun shine:
Why don't you just come back to bed?

WAITING FOR SOMEONE AT THE BAR

two guys behind me at bar:
there was an oncoming car
a stop
with sideswipe fender bender
the other driver was dumbstruck
clearly out of it
must have been at least 70
clearly an Alzheimer
like my father
the witness to the witness said

I wanted to say
the guy was clearly
out of it
yes
out of your limited range
maybe on his way to a date
with someone of his age
or older

what do you young self-righteous
drunks
know about us
people over seventy?

and besides how do you know it wasn't
your friend who had veered over the line and
started yelling and screaming at
the dumbstruck older guy?

that's what I felt like saying to the voices
behind me
but I didn't
I was busy watching the door
and hoping that the person I was waiting for
would not run into a brash
thirty-something accident

THE SECOND COMING OF ANTICHRIST

when she takes too much antidepressant
at dusk auntie Anne
lying back on her Victorian sofa
tends to see Antichrist
climb over the antimacassar
toting his taut anti-crucifix

she calls out to him: Antichrist!
          Antichrist!
praying for an anticlimax has worn me out
but I'll do it
if you really want to come again

LOIS BARR

BOTANIC GARDEN WALTZ FOR SENIORS

Will I come to the gardens
On a day like today?
When I'm wrinkled and achy,
Will I walk with a cane?

Will we come to the gardens
on a day that's so fine?
Will I push your wheelchair,
Or will you push mine?

With a floppy straw hat
I'll be leaky or lame.
You'll walk ten steps ahead.
Will I still know your name?

All the weeds will be trimmed.
All dead blooms clipped away.
Will I come to the gardens
On a day like today?

The hedges pruned neatly
Their angles so true.
The geese will fly over
In a sky cobalt blue.

Will I come to the gardens
When the roses bloom?
Will you come to the gardens?
And will I walk with you?

MARALEE GERKE

THE PHYSICS OF TIME

Neck deep in clouds of
lavender scented bubbles
I close my eyes and
muse on the physics of time.

The pull of gravity
that widens my hips,
compels my breasts to sag,
thrusts the riparian corridors
of my body earthward.

Scars displayed on
my flaccid belly;
proof that I have conquered
significant mountains.

Weighed down,
heat weak, dizzy
I rise from the bath
and rub a worn pink towel
over my changed body.

I need no mirror to show me
the effects of life's passage.
I am a witness to my own demise.
A life lived in the certainty of mortality.

Then you enter the steamy room,
cup my breast and bury
your mouth in my still wet hair,
I smile. As long as you are here
there is still time.

ELISAVIETTA RITCHIE

FOR A JEALOUS SUITOR, GETTING ON

"The verb to love has no past tense."
Konstantin Simonov

I mention old lovers. You envision
wheelchairs, walkers and canes, a battalion
who bob, hawk and hobble up my worn stairs,
saliva ignored on their bird-nest beards.

A properly comic scene. Not yet true
but I trust my seasoned loves will endure
as they do now, across oceans and years
alive in my mind, and now haunting yours.

The best of my lot are already dead.
"The body's tyranny," one artist said.
Not sure then which part he meant, now I find
the body's treachery outstrips the mind's.

So I'm relieved your eyesight's feebler than
your memory. And glad you're still on hand.

ONE WEDDING NIGHT

He blinks to note the old
woman parked in his bed, all

wrinkles and bellies, breasts
not as full as they seemed.

Which psychological drive, she
wonders, pushed her to sleep

with this grandfather figure,
and what if, in the midst

of things, his heart fails?
What would the rescue squad—

those husky bucks—speculate?
Not the usual bimbo here

who makes an old man's pump
seize up when he tries—

He turns down, she turns
off, the unkind light.

In silence they strive
to ignore imperfections,

remember the rules, or
at least work around them,

holding each other
lightly as luna moths.

AS AFTER A THIRTY-YEARS' WAR: OLD LOVERS

They remember every word we spoke, our
smoked oysters, rum balls, coffee *mit schlag,* served
with sweet promises of love eternal
when they moved on. For like rivers they are

always in flux, though some dry up. We plod
dusty wadis through deserts, but glance back
over our shoulders should the current lack
of lovers turn into a sudden flood.

Yes! Old codgers trickle in, then waves flow
toward our doors. Yet bloated, or bony, shrunk...
white-bristled billy goats. Bunioned hooves clunk
over our thresholds. Still hungry, they know

we are a soft touch. They were our soul mates
once. Now, we confront our doubles, our fate.

PATRICIA SULLIVAN

LOVE AFTER SEVENTY

We were winding down the end of a week that had been by turn rainy, snowy, blustery and just plain freezing. A few mild January days had lulled us into complacency, a hope that winter might not come this year. What? A survivor of seventy-six New England winters and I still don't know that Massachusetts is unpredictability at its worst? We have known unseasonal warmth in mid-February, only to be knocked down by an April blizzard. My husband says you have to be crazy to live in New England.

After hours of weather induced close proximity, we began to snap at each other, to chafe at our differences. At seventy-four, Paul has become more of a pessimist than ever. In these later years I have left behind my usual cautious optimism for a solid dose of realism. As a former math teacher, he views life as a lesson in black and white. I am more inclined to see it as a blur of pinks and grays. While he sees the eternal glass half empty, no, I don't see the optimist's half full. I tell him it's just half a glass of water.

Even in frigid weather he bundles up for daily walks; one mid-morning, a second walk in late afternoon. I prefer to huddle in the warmth of our family room, reaching for a lap blanket and a good book. He says I'm becoming a hothouse flower. I'm not. I'm hibernating.

The weather broke on Saturday, temperatures rose to a tolerable degree and at Paul's urging we headed out for a hike through nearby park land, accessing a tract owned and maintained by the local Valley Trust. A clearly marked trail, but the footing was slow and unsure. Often our boots disappeared into deep patches of snow and we were forced to reach for each other to avoid falling.

Trudging through the quiet woods, the absence of sound was almost a sound in itself. Only an occasional bird interrupted as we made our way up and down the snow covered hills in healing silence. From time to time we stopped to turn our faces toward the sun, drawing sustenance from this unexpected warmth, something we hadn't felt for each other in days. We walked, we looked, we appreciated. Near trail's end, a roaring of cars on the interstate highway broke our mood. "Close your eyes," he said. "It sounds like the ocean!" He was right. Surely that was the pounding of a wild surf! Then, back up the road, across a sprawling field, returning at last to the warmth of our small house and perhaps to the warmth of each other.

The past week's low-key life had invited an intricate jigsaw puzzle to take shape on the dining room table. It was a difficult puzzle, a many shaded picture of fruits and vegetables, stalks and leaves waiting to be matched together with patience. It occurred to me that we spend a lot of time looking for the right pieces to fit the puzzles of our own lives. In those rare times when we find them, and redefine them, we can count ourselves lucky.

CLAUDETTE MORK SIGG

DIVERGENCE IN FLIGHT

You fed on fire;
I fed on you, and though we started out
going in the same direction—
you turning yourself clockwise
around whatever images that came your way—
I found myself—I don't know how it happened—
going the other way.

Now, as we circle—gliding like birds
from one branch to another in trees we have claimed,
yours bristly gray pines, half-dead,
growing defiantly in dolomite;
mine sun-baked desert palms rooted
in the subterranean sands of a creeping fault—
our lives careen past each other on contrary paths,
miles apart.

Two lovers who started together
but diverged in a long moment's blink, we
hardly know what to signal to each other
across the distance.

Only the color of your skin,
translucent with images I once knew,
tells me we once loved each other,
the fire we fed on having flowed from the same spring.

WHAT MY HUSBAND DISCARDED

The filing cabinet is filled with dead things, discards, fragments
no longer viable, remnants of who we were: in the top drawer,
decades of Ashland itineraries, Shakespearean dramas,
life-shadows once important. Folders filled with trips
we never took: Delphi and the oracle whose message
about my life I never heard, riddle though it would have been.
Mistakes of love fermenting in a folder filled with
complaints—why don't you love me as I love you?

Mimeographed copies of the myth "Enki and Ninhursag,"
too precious to throw away, never read now, but lingering
as a passion that reached out into desert wastes
before dying in the heat of a hot Mesopotamian sun.
Investments—Occidental Land Research—that evaporated
like a well depleted before even dug. The folder on menopause,
hot flashes, arthritic joints, thinning hair, liver spots
on a once clear complexion—present and accepted.

The oak filing cabinet, too heavy, solid as a tree,
forsaken—and me. Oh, yes, me, too, discarded
when he walked out the door, leaving his key
on the kitchen table next to his empty coffee cup.

LIKE LOVE

The rain clouds are crowding against the Sierras.
If they know anything, they know they want to rise,
to rush with hurricane winds battering
their thunderous backsides, to let torrents flow
and then ice up with snow on an earth gone frigid.
They want desert and sunrise,
the unknowing nothingness that will free them
from what they can't help—
                                        like love, sneaking
around a corner, waiting for you to come
with your innocent eyes, looking for nothing
but the moment's music, and there he is,
nothing at all, but there at the right time—
and you are lost to someone you never wanted at all.

SONDRA ZEIDENSTEIN

ANOTHER COUNTRY

I often wonder how Iraqis or Palestinians or Israelis go about their lives
          among snipers and bombers,
how they get out of bed every morning, plan the day's meals, shop,
send the husband, uncle, child to carry on what each day requires
when there's so much risk.
I've moved into a world of danger now.
It's called old age.
Any headache or bloating can signal a last illness, nothing secure,
each touch of my love at night
heated with the joy of being together and the sorrow of ending.
How do *I* get up in the morning, sit on the shaded deck,
watch for jay or cardinal, become distracted
by long-legged hornets at the edge of the deck,
two of them, striped yellow and brown,
one lying totally still, the other walking around it,
nudging the still one's antennae.
Here is the news of the day,
this gentle shoving against an inert body with a threadlike leg.
Is it a funeral rite?
I would have longed to perform such a rite over my sister,
patient, curious, licking sweat and salt crystallized on her cold, cold body.
Even after the lifeless hornet begins to stir,
its companion keeps prodding, lying on top of it
until, can I believe my eyes? it shudders, wakes, moves,
is enticed, I imagine, to live,
warmed, as I am in the night, by a comrade.
Is that why I lie sleeping in early morning, my husband tells me,
          with a smile on my face?

Am I cheered by our ankles entwined, the touch of his toes,
his heated belly pressing my hip?
By sunny afternoon, a dozen hornets buzz sluggishly,
the coddled one I'm sure a part of their number,
all the legs dangling like ladders under a rescue helicopter,
all the small fat bodies gleaming.

SECRET LIFE

How studied I was in my adultery,
so much purpose in the hour I had
after the children left for school
and my husband for work,
transforming myself for my lover.
The big thing, when I showered,
my pin curls guarded by an ample cap,
was not to wet my hair.
Legs shaved smooth and muscle-glossy.
Fine silk garter belt, half slip, unpadded bra.
Well shaped feet in supple pumps.
Ah! Five feet eight.
The children by now at PS 122,
I concentrate on deodorant,
the wash of toner and base,
eyebrows examined for strays,
mascara, eyeliner, careful now!
to spread long lashes without clotting.
Shiny tube of lipstick in manicured fingers.
Gold hoops, always the hoops,
to look provocative. Breath held
in the narrow bathroom, I release
each bobby pin from its skull-denting hold,
and feel myself slide out of everyday life,
as I do now, picking raspberries in October
after frost:
       Don't lose one soft, plump, purply,
almost sweet fruit from between the fingers,
loud, sluggish, autumn bees alerting me
to guard my reach.

Brushing it then,
my hair, the part exactly straight, out and under,
trying for a page boy, smooth,
like the underside of a cresting wave
that will be dashed by the time I come back home,
key in the lock, will be lank and straight,
sweat-damp at the neck, as I sit with my daughter
for cookies and milk.
So far away that time,
the secret my week circled. Now, often,
before dawn, my skin drawing heat
from my husband's like a furnace, so intense,
I lie awake grieving how lost
one of us will be forever from the other, one day.

JUNE 25, 2007

on my son's fifty-first birthday

I barely made it up
the long blank steps
of the hospital's
desolate concrete,
wheel-chaired in a hurry
through sickly green halls
to a windowless room
with no hint of June's bounty.
8 a.m. I gave him birth,
squat, squashed-faced,
bright red in the hard heart
of downtown.
                      When he gets home
from work I'll call him,
my son in a mill town house
in Maine, a low, broad hillside,
baby birds twittering
as they do here in the tame woods
of Connecticut,
catbird squawking,
pale-pink peonies wide open,
first four-petaled magenta flowers
on stalks of loosestrife,
foxglove bending under
their loads of blossoms,
the chill already gone,
moist green life holding us,
on this knuckled planet,

the light so long
I can't reach its stretch
with my fingertips.
Let it kiss the afternoon
darkened cheek of my son.
How we love each other
across the hills, our kindness
and hard work.

CONNECTION

What do I write back to an old lover who has e-mailed me after thirty
years, he 73 and I
            74 and three quarters,
wanting to meet me for coffee in the city, at Starbucks, to connect. "So
much water
            under the bridge (cliché)," he writes.

Just as well he doesn't say "reconnect," since I don't know who he is now
and I,
            for sure,
am not the sexy young academic, muscular ass in a miniskirt, who,
constantly between
            her legs,

felt luscious and itchy. I am not that woman who must have wounded him
when I said
            (big lie),
I was going to become monogamous again and so would not even kiss
him,

certainly not invite him over once a week to study for our orals, the
housekeeper,
            with a knowing smile,
leaving early, the children in school. I'm not that woman anymore, though
I so easily
            tease into silk panties and thin silk bra remembering her.

Smug, she had no heart, that woman on her Williamsburg bedspread, in
stockings and
            garter belt,
who said "I love you" after and held him close.

Would I be shocked at how old he is (even if he is working out), afraid of
            his seeing how old I am?

Would I wear my partial denture or let him see the gap, dark, at the side of my
        mouth when I smile?

Would he wear toner on his cheeks (like me), smell of something after-
shavy?
Would we have thought long about what we cannot say

unless I say first: let me tell you the truth.
Let me tell you, back then I hadn't been born yet.

I've put in years to change the very circuits of my brain. Who are you?
I can't travel all that way: car to train station, train to the city, bus to the
crowded room,
        small table, the latte, foam on my very thin upper lip,

unless I am willing to tell you I lied. We can go on from there.

But if I did travel to the city to meet you again
after thirty years: your black, sephardic-curly hair,
dark eyes, your face shadowy but full of smiles
and easy laughter, someone who could tell a funny story,
someone who was always flirting, but surprised
to find yourself in bed with a woman not your wife,
someone boyish, oblivious to how a woman
feels pleasure, someone always pleased with yourself,
if we did meet again after thirty years, why would I want
to hurt your feelings? After all, your mouth had been soft
against mine, I'd entered your arms with trust, we'd been
young, friends. Why would I want affection to splatter
on the rickety table with the latte? Wouldn't I rather be left,
still a liar, but holding something sweet and fragrant,
something salvaged, to be savored in our hearts.

MARILYNN DUNHAM

NOW THAT WE ARE OLD

Dr. Stillwell's Stay Well Newsletter had arrived that day. Kitty read it as she munched on her sardine sandwich with spicy mustard. "Hmmm," she said as she turned the page.

"What?" Joe looked up from the financial section of the newspaper. "What cha reading?"

"Dr. Stillwell says that just ten minutes of sun during the peak time of the day—between ten in the morning and four PM won't hurt you. He says that the benefits you get from the Vitamin D, for strong bones, will outweigh any danger from the UV rays."

"Well, I don't know," worried Joe, "how can you be sure that's true? Don't want you to get skin cancer."

She pushed herself back from the table and stood, stretched her back and smiled at him, "If Dr. Stillwell says it's so—it's so."

"Yeah, yeah, I know about you and Dr. Stillwell," Joe said. He smiled and gave her a light pat on her knee.

Kitty looked at the wall clock, it was just after noon. "This is peak time now. I'm going to do it." She thought for a minute and looked outside the kitchen window. "I know, I'll go behind the pump house so no one will see me."

"Why? You mean you're going to be naked out there?"

"Why not? No one will see me. Hey, I'm eighty, and I have osteoporosis. I have to do everything I can to stay well, now that I'm old."

"Well. Hon. You are taking calcium, magnesium and Vitamin D."

"Yeah," she glanced at the remains of her sandwich, "and I am eating these poor little sardines—all smushed together in that oily little can."

First she went into their bedroom to get the alarm clock, then into the garage where she stripped off her clothes, and dropped them on the floor. She felt strange walking across their yard naked, but it felt kind of daring too. The grass was deep and cool and she stopped to scrunch her bare toes into the clover. A bee on a small pink blossom fluttered its see thru' wings. She could feel the fresh and exhilarating breeze on her neck; down her back and on her bottom as she leaned down to see the bee.

She began humming SWEET GEORGIA BROWN and did a little dance on her way to the pump house. It was perfectly safe here—very private—they lived on a hill and visitors had to drive up a steep driveway to get to their house and their neighbors were fields away. Behind the pump house she set the clock down on a stump, in plain sight, to be sure to stay only ten minutes. The sun beamed warm upon her face. She stretched her arms out wide, up to the sky. Warm. It felt warm. Delicious. About that time two Ravens flew by. They circled back and came down closer, and then they were gone. She laughed to herself and imagined that one Raven said, "Now, what in theeeee hell was that?" But then she thought it might also have said, "How lovely."

Joe still sat at the kitchen table with the newspaper spread out in front of him but he couldn't concentrate. All he could think of was the Sun Goddess behind the pump house. At last he gave in, stood up and stepped out of his slippers, his socks, pants, boxer shorts, unbuttoned his shirt, pulled it off and headed out the door.

"Yoo Hoo," he crooned as he stepped around to the back of the pump house, "any naked women around here?"

She screamed but when she saw him standing there with his knobby knees and dimpled belly she started to giggle.

"Oh, Honey, aren't you just too cute?"

"And you, my love," he said in his sexiest voice as he came near to her and wrapped her in his arms.

"But, how will I get any sun?"

"First this," he cupped her breast in his hand, pulled it up and began to nibble.

But at that very moment a small truck drove into the driveway. Kitty and Joe heard someone get out and knock on their front door. Then they heard, "Mr. Bates, hello, anyone home?" Someone inside the truck said something—they couldn't hear what, and then the person at their door said, "Yeah, I know they're home—look the garage door's open, God, I hope they're all right."

Now they heard the other door open and a new voice said, "Let's look in the garage."

"Amazing," said the first voice, "there's a stack of women's clothes laying here on the floor—something's wrong."

Kitty whispered, "we've got to get out of this sun!"

Joe looked down at his body, he pressed himself against the pump house wall for balance and stuck his head around the corner. "Hello, over here at the pump house."

The two men looked his way. "Mr. Bates? We're here from Smooth Flo Septic Systems—to service your septic system. Is everything all right?"

"Yes, of course everything's all right. Don't you usually call first?"

"Sorry, we were down the road at the Jensen's—in the neighborhood—you know? We thought we'd just come on up."

"Yeah, well you can just get your sorry ass back in your truck and get the hell out of here." He waited for a moment, took a deep breath, and then yelled, "Call for an appointment." He looked at Kitty. Her titties bounced when she gave him two thumbs up.

The truck drove away. Warm pee trickled down Kitty's thighs she was laughing so hard.

"Hey, let's go have some tea." She said.

They hurried across the yard. Joe grabbed her hand to steady her. They had to get out of the sun. It had now been fifteen minutes.

"I want some of that spicy kind," Joe said.

"Spicy? Oh yes, the spicy green tea. In one of his newsletters Dr. Stillwell says that green tea contains powerful antioxidants. I'll have some too." She squeezed his hand, "We've got to do everything we can to stay well, you know, now that we're old."

IT IS YOUR BIRTHDAY

Theodore Brownlee sat upright in bed after doing the exercises the physical therapist had taught him years before. He believed in them. Well, he was ninety-two and still moving. That spoke for something. When both feet were firmly planted on the floor he walked to the bathroom and looked at the calendar on the wall. "Lets see," he mumbled as he studied hard at the calendar. Yes, this was Monday, the twenty-fourth of April, and it was the Lady's birthday. He could hear her in the other room crooning to the cat, Kitty Blue. In her high shrilly voice, "How do you do, Kitty Blue?" over and over. Some days to be perfectly honest it got on his nerves, but not this morning, because it was her birthday and they were going on an outing.

At breakfast they made their plans to go immediately after lunch and before naptime. Mr. Brownlee wanted the old Cadillac to be spruced up for his Lady so he filled a bucket with hot vinegar water, found some rags and the classified section from the Sunday newspaper. He was a retired navy man and knew the right way to clean the windshield. He turned on the engine when the windshield was clean. It was running like a top. He smiled as he wiped off the passenger seat—where the Lady would ride to the card shop.

Later at Isobella's Card and Gift Shoppe he stood by the birthday card display. He had remembered to wear his glasses so he could read each verse and admire the artwork. The Lady wandered around the store looking and occasionally he could hear her chuckle. About thirty minutes passed before Theodore called her over. He placed his favorite one in her hand. "This is for you," he said softly.

The Lady took it in her white and very wrinkled hands and read the front; she paused for a moment and then opened it slowly and read the message inside. She pulled it into her chest. "Thank you, Dear One," her eyes filled with tears.

All he could say was, "You're welcome."

They stood there quietly in their moment.

Then she handed it to him, he placed it back on the shelf, and they walked arm in arm out of the card shop.

One year later.

After cleaning the windshield on the cad and dusting off the seats he started it to make sure it was still running. The card shop looked the same—just as he'd remembered it. He stood for a long time reading the cards and he smiled as he read, chuckled once, and dabbed his eyes with his monogrammed handkerchief. When he'd found the perfect card he brought it to his chest and whispered, "This one's for you," and held the silence while his Lady received it.

But something happened when he started to put it back, and Mr. Theodore Brownlee walked to the cashier, took out his wallet and put down a five-dollar bill. The cashier, a young man, asked if he wanted a bag. "No thank you," he replied and slid it into his inside vest pocket where he'd once carried pink and white mints for the grandchildren.

ALEXANDRINA SERGIO

AT THE SUPERMARKET: SHOPPING FOR THE BASICS

I like old guys with ponytails
And young ones lank and thin as rails
Who ease on past the produce stands
Giant juice jars in both hands.

I do enjoy the dark skinned youth
Who flexes at the courtesy booth,
Piercing eyes and high boned cheek
Like god both African and Greek.

I make my way by salad dressing,
Smiling to myself, confessing
How nice again at soda rack
To see the chap with hair tied back.

When no way can I grasp the bleach
Stacked up so high beyond my reach
I tell the gent who helps me out
He's shining knight without a doubt.

And when the bags are all packed in
By sweet old man with twinkling grin
I head for home, hopes ratified:
This shopping trip has satisfied.

What? I forgot your damson jam?
Your pitted prunes? Your can of Spam?
Oh please forgive me, Dearest Love.
What could I have been thinking of?

HONORING MY MOTHER

I always park in the same place at the mall
To enter Macy's on a straight path to Perfume
Where I pretend-study the offerings
And when unobserved
Spray my wrists, behind my ears, even my coat,
Mime a frown, inhale the back of my hand.

You played no such apologetic charade.
With panache you would make the rounds
To G. Fox, Brown Thompson, Sage-Allen, Steiger's;
Lift glittering atomizers to your throat, hair,
Fill the air with a delirious fragrance
That followed as you walked on to more mundane tasks.

Perfumers of the world would not approve your mix,
But a little girl thought you always smelled most wonderful.

I park in the same space,
Head through the store
Straight to you.

REMEMBERING OUR NAMES

I chide him for keeping the battered old rolodex.
"Most everyone in it is dead or gone,"
I tell him, "and besides, it's too big."

I reach to put it with the trash,
But he opens it and reads the names out,
Queenie,
Mary,
Joe,
Good neighbors long moved on.
Uncle George,
Aunt Kate,
Ken, my sweet funny cousin,
Lois,
Dead, all, for years.
Pete,
Ron,
Ellie,
Dear friends absorbed by time and distance.

I put the rolodex back on the shelf,
Each well fingered card
A record of love,
A faded piece of the puzzle
Of who we are.

LUCILLE GANG SHULKLAPPER

AND WHAT IMPORTANCE DO I HAVE IN THE COURTROOM OF OBLIVION?

Title after Neruda

I have this much: Sammy said, "I love you,"
slipping the handle from the open door,
holding his seven-year-old shoulders high,
straw hair uncombed, loose teeth unbrushed, parents
away, away-o. I am his lifeline.
I have evidence. Breakfast crumbs from his
toast, stains from cracked eggs, fragmented shells,
an empty plate. Proof of a grandmother's love.

I have a cat book, curled-up pages, a
pummeled pillow, two swimming towels, sweat socks,
a tee shirt with the shark from *Jaws*. I keep
bottled water on ice in the freezer.
In the decay of memory, I will
summon love. In my trial, it is all.

SEND IN THE WORMS: A LOVE STORY

In the entrance way of The Oasis Funeral Home, my husband Al and I pause in front of the copper-plated sign: Dignity. "It must be off-season," I laugh, turning my back to the sign. "Look at all those polished hearses standing in line like taxi cabs."

Once inside, the telephone rings with controlled quiet. As the pre-needs counselor, Bertha Toles, approaches us in a long flowing black dress, I poke my husband, and laugh sotto voce. "There's a dress code here."

"Stop it, Lu," my husband says under his breath. "Cut it OUT!"

Bertha seats herself behind a massive desk and gestures toward two overstuffed chairs. There's a vase on the shelf behind her and I wonder if someone's remains are in it.

"Is that a pre-owned urn?" I ask.

My husband glowers.

Bertha giggles. "No, but we have a display room. Do you want to be cremated?"

"Yes." I quickly answer.

"And you, Al?"

"No." My husband gives me one of his exasperated looks. "Where would I visit you if you're cremated? I want to be next to you."

"My mother had a special lining in her casket," I continue. "That's why I want to be cremated. "She didn't want worms to get inside."

Bertha pulls a tissue from her sleeve. "*Do you know anyone who says, 'send in the worms'?*"

Then, Bertha hands us a checklist of services and prices. "Will you stay in Florida, Al, if Lucille dies first?"

"Yes."

"Lucille?"

"No. Part of the year, I'd live near my family in Virginia."

"Don't count on that," my husband says. "They could move to

Alaska."

I can tell I'm going to be buried in the ground in Florida. There's no special lining but a cement burial vault so the casket doesn't sink into the water or get washed away in hurricane season. "O.K. I won't burn or drown. The worms are winning."

"Refrigeration or embalming?"

"Graveside service, chapel, or combination?"

"Prepay the rabbi?"

We're on a roll now. Both of us nodding and agreeing while Bertha rings up items faster than the scanner at the grocery store. We only hesitate in the display room. Our pre-need caskets are displayed like pre-owned cars; the most expensive ones first. It would cost more than $20,000 to keep the worms out.

Bertha has one casket rolled into the display room from the back. She opens it carefully, peers inside. "Have to make sure no one's in it."

It's buckeye and has a Jewish star to match that can be stuck on or not like in a sticker book. My husband and I will have matching caskets. Two steps up from plain pine with holes drilled in the bottom to let the worms in as fast as they can crawl.

"Should we take the hearse to the cemetery?" Bertha jokes.

"It's not a bad drive," my husband says when we arrive.

Bertha drives us around the burial "gardens." There are scattered trees at planned points, and inscribed benches instead of headstones.

"What are those buildings?" I ask.

"Those are mausoleums," Bertha tells us.

"I've never seen a mausoleum before."

Bertha stops the car. We stand in front of an above the ground concrete bunker, like a filing cabinet for dead bodies. "Heart level," Bertha says, pointing to the second tier, "costs the most. Eye-level's the next. You can be buried in tandem, head to toe or side by side. Side by side costs more."

The sun is beating down on me, on one bunch of wilted flowers, and on a pile of pebbles at the base to show that someone has visited. *Who were they for?*

"If you die first, I don't want to stand in front of a cement block," my husband says. "Let's go look at the next available "garden." I'd like a tree and a bench. "

He has the funniest way of saying 'I love you.'

I love him so much.

"Send in the worms," I say.

MYRNA GOODMAN

PREPARATIONS

Next to the fish store
a man about seventy
turned rich spring earth
with tools from the old country.
Spadefuls lifted, put down,
lifted again, put down.
Each week, from May
to September, shopping
for salmon or shrimp,
I watched him from my car.
Sweaty, on strong knees
he thinned lettuce, picked peas,
talked to himself in Italian
staking tomatoes, plucking
grapes from a tumbledown trellis.
Later, preparing my dinner,
drinking white wine,
I imagined his wife in an apron
washing lettuce, stirring sauce,
setting his place just so.
This summer weeds and leaves
cover the earth: his spade against
a tree, his widow at the window.

A GOOD MAN IS HARD TO FIND

For Flannery O'Connor and Jane Flanders

They took his name
off the white wall
in the reception hall;
one letter at a time
released
from thirty years of bonding.
First the G, then the O, and so
and so until all that was left
was the pale twin of GOODMAN.

He brought the letters home.

A practice merges—a man's
name is written off.
I don't believe him when
he says it doesn't matter;
yet I love him for his lie.

I spend my morning moving
seven capital letters
around the kitchen table.
GOOD
GOD
DAMN
DOOM
MAD
MAN
GOODMAN

TIME AND TIDE

...it could happen any day now, just like that—any day. E. L. *2004*

Some day soon, dear friend, the time
will come when one of us, probably me
because I'm four years younger,

or you, since you're so much stronger,
will take the other by the hand:
first straighten her coat collar, then

wipe the tiny crumbs accumulated
on the lower lip, *don't forget your glasses,*
careful on the steps out to the old red car.

Off we'll go, not on some adventure in the City
or class at the Print Center, or painting trees
in Katonah, not out to your rose garden to smoke

pot or down to my studio to coil pots,
but to a bench in a park near Greenwich
by the water's edge (which always calms us.)

Two old women sharing a sandwich, ceaselessly
talking as the tide rolls in. First you, then me,
and, as always, both at the same time.

Mascara melting, we'll laugh and laugh.
We would still do that. Brooklyn and Wisconsin,
together laughing, as the tide teeters.

IN SICKNESS AND HEALTH

SYLVIE TERESPOLSKI

WHAT'S IT ALL ABOUT, KETZEL?

I was at the hospital visiting a friend of fifty years, Ketzel, who just had quadruple bypass surgery after she suffered a heart attack and as people are wont to do when they've had a close call she began to tear up as I sat by her bedside. She took my hand and softly said, "You're so beautiful and smart and kind, I can't understand why you never found someone to love you after your divorce."

I said nothing because I found myself in semi-shock. This topic had never come up between us and I sat there bristling at what I interpreted as pity and an erroneous perspective. My being alone after my divorce twenty-seven years ago and after a miserable twenty-six-year marriage never struck me as a particularly unfortunate situation. Many people live with tons of loneliness even if they live with someone or a bunch of people and I had long ago concluded that fear of being alone was the number one reason that people got together after propagating years were over. I guess my silence sent the message that she should continue. "Do you ever think about it?"

I remained mute because I couldn't tell her what I really mused about while she was struggling between the here and the ever after. One cannot start the eighth decade of life without being aware of the certainty of death. At this stage, I am more than ever aware of the hangman's noose and I certainly didn't want to answer her with death on my mind. In one year, I lost nine acquaintances, six women and three men. While they were not necessarily part of my daily life, they were present at some time in my story. Most were my contemporary—some a bit older or younger. Sometime in the recent present, I had talked to them and was deeply aware of their existence and suddenly my once-in-a-while lunch date, or "here's a good book to read" adviser is gone. No possibility of telephone calls, dates for coffee, laughs, tears, remembrances.

I didn't tell my friend lying there with fluid in her lungs and oxygen feeders that my most powerful musing lately is how is "it" going to happen?

And the "it" is not "love." Cancer, heart, stroke, Alzheimer's anyone? The statistics are enough to make one less than cheerful. If you live to be 85, your chances are one in three that you'll develop Alzheimer's. I read the obituaries in *The New York Times* searching for clues for longevity especially when I see someone, a perfect stranger close to my age of 73. How did they live their lives that brought about their premature death? At least, I consider death in one's seventies premature. I'm a bit smug with the silent answer. Surely, with my good living of exercise, proper diet, I will have a longer healthier expectancy than they did. The limitations? What will the limitations be? Diminished eyesight, hearing, flexibility, strength, toughness? Diminished, diminished, diminished. Even worse, people will have diminished expectations and automatically put you into the "old lady" slot.

Right now, I'm just a bit slower on the "Jeopardy" questions and the crossword puzzle answers. The responses are on the tip of my tongue but the synapses don't connect immediately. Maybe a split second later or maybe at 2:00 a.m., I'll remember that George Fox founded the Quakers or that the Congo is the longest semi-circular river in Africa, or that Dylan's other name is Zimmerman.

A lot really to think about—the unknown, the somewhat scary, the "out of your hands" events in your life.

Eventually, I found enough voice to say to her, "How could I not think about love? It's everywhere. I mean everywhere and the majority of it is about carnal cravings." (I'm writing this as *Sex and the City* is being distributed worldwide.) "I wonder if anyone ever did a scientific study of what we learned by osmosis—just by flicking the radio dial, seeing a newspaper headline, hearing an advertisement for a movie, watching the world of people walk by on a Sunday afternoon in the park, reading a book.

"Where would Alfred Hitchcock's movie, *Notorious* be without those gorgeous love scenes between Cary Grant and Ingrid Bergman? I know younger people might find their models in today's romantic comedies but no contemporary movie says it better than those scenes between Cary Grant and Ingrid Bergman, or Ingrid Bergman with Humphrey Bogart. With all their clothes on their love was palpable and could reach out from the screen and touch your heart and you would say to yourself, 'I want that. Whatever it is they're having, I want it.' I said that before that line became famous in *When Harry Met Sally*."

Ketzel struggled with her breathing. "You're changing the subject. I know you know a lot about the movies. I'm talking about you and finding someone—some nice guy who deserves you. And I'm not talking about high drama. This is not an *Antony and Cleopatra* conversation." She always had a way of making her points invoking literature.

"Look," I said. "As I've gotten more mature (older) I've seen love in film that's less about lust and more about—well—unusual combinations of people. *Harold and Maude, Lost in Translation, Away from Her,* and *Guarding Tess.* People who really touched one another emotionally who took up good space in each other's lives, who contributed to other's well-being in some way, who looked forward to being with one another because their spirits were boosted just by the sheer presence of the other, or maybe the sheer knowledge that this person was in their lives."

"So...." She lengthens the "o" trying to make the conversation continue without much effort on her part. She is very tired but I know she is contemplating. She regains some strength. "There's the love that one sees between a man and a woman who have been together for a long time. They're in their eighties and when they grab for each other's hand, dust the dandruff off the shoulder or when the man gently tucks a lock of hair back behind the ear of his partner, you can't deny that's wonderful to behold."

"Don't say anymore," I tell her. "I'm not denying the beauty of that kind of intimacy but I have never had it and I never expect to get it." My voice had risen in annoyance.

"Don't get angry," she said. "We'll talk more. I'm tired." She closed her eyes.

I left with my arguments running around in my thoughts. She had really gotten to me and the rebuttals began to play in my head. People who live alone do this a lot.

What if you really like being alone? Not all the time but manage your solitude really well and are delighted when you leave the luncheon, or the party, or the lecture and crawl into your own bed happily alone so you can decide whether to turn on the light switch and continue reading or just pull the covers up over your head and meditate yourself to dreamland. You don't really rely on someone else for your conversational or sexual pleasure— you really can do most of it yourself and the list of plumbers/handymen rests right on your nightstand—for home repairs, naturally—the critical telephone numbers for single homeowners. You even manage movies, theatres, parties, and a dozen sundry events by yourself. You keep a hammer and a cell phone under your pillow and feel totally secure after double bolting all the doors and windows.

She, my friend Ketzel of fifty years lying in the hospital bed might ask if I ever get lonely. I will tell her what I've told all those others who have asked. "Haven't you ever been lonely even with a partner by your side?" That is not unusual between us—answering a question with a question and all is understood.

Besides, I recognize that there is love in so many places. I pick up the four-and-a-half-year-old grandson at pre-school and surprise him with a visit telling him I'm going to take him home to my house to bake cookies. He looks at me with wide eyes. "Past Michael's dinner? Will I stay with you past Michael's dinner?" (His younger brother.) When I say, "Yes," I get a huge hug that almost knocks me over as I squat down next to him. An unbelievable feeling of love? You betcha.

And then, my kids in their forties call me periodically—not to tell me how much they love me. That would not work for this family but they give me updates on their lives because they know how much we mean to each other. No mushy telephone messages. No hearts and flowers. Just practical updates, e.g, how they're doing in new relationships, the diagnosis of one grandhild is ADD, not autism, a question about how to cook a roast. I guess those needs are a vital part of the "loving" process but from what I've learned from the past, it's got to be a healthy "need." It can't be "neediness."

My children also grow up and the second time fall in love with the right person. They learned from their mistakes. I can remember the day I told my daughter I was so proud of her, not for all her accomplishments in her teens and twenties and there were many of them, but in her forties when she turned her life around and made a much better companion choice in her life. Maybe selfishly I loved her too much that day because the second choice in a mate reflected more of my values. I can't deny it.

I experience love when I ask my fourteen-year-old granddaughter what author she is reading and she gives me the put down stare. "I don't read authors. I read *genres*." The reality that this teenage child with her red pantyhose and polka dot skirt and multi-colored tennis shoes is growing up to be her own person just overwhelms me to tears of love and frustration.

Then there is the love that is linked to an addiction. People hear that word and they cringe because it conjures up all sorts of negative images.

Really negative images. But my particular addiction is beautiful because it allows you to float on the surfaces of the water and have an integral, holistic, authentic experience with your mind, body, and the natural world around you. I have become addicted to sculling or rowing. I search the weather report daily sometimes twice, three times a day to check the weather conditions because that's my first priority in the daily scheme of things. Get out there and push your body, focus your mind to finish a head race, to compete in a 1000 meter race in your single, to row in a double with your partner as though you're Fred Astaire and Ginger Rogers. In short, although you do it well, you want to do it better. There are always seconds to shave off your time, form to improve. Just make sure the wind isn't gusting and the water and air temperature will allow you to survive if you take a spill in your boat that you have facetiously named "Two to Tango."

My friend will say to me, "I am talking about people, not sports. You know I hate sports."

I will tell her that there could be a book *Loving Beyond People*. I love rowing—it consumes me and I give it a lot of time and attention. I love reading books that consume me—that absorb me—that take me to another world. I can say the same for theatre and movies—a piece of music—*Carmen Burina, Redi Pagliacci, Seasons of Love* from *Rent*. I can love a moment when all seems fused together in a right way—not to create a "Perfect Storm" but simply a "Perfectly Lovely and Loving Moment." Is it the same as loving another human being as in a love relationship? I don't know, but it's got to be close.

I go back to the hospital for another visit with Ketzel and I am armed with my arguments. She is paler and she tells me that they have upped the oxygen. She summons the energy to ask about kids, grandkids, and even my rowing addiction. I share anecdotes with her. The nurse comes around to check her blood pressure; she tells me that my friend didn't sleep well last night. I squeeze her hand and say I'll be back tomorrow.

Ketzel, my friend of fifty years doesn't have the energy to squeeze back but she whispers, "I love you."

"I know," I say trying to keep my voice from quivering.

I leave with love, death, and life all confounded in my thoughts and know that I will never sort it out. I just have to let it be.

DOROTHY STONE

TETHERED

The tube
snakes up the stairs
follows you
wherever you go.
I follow you too
keeping it
away from your ankles.
No coiled tangle needed
to make you trip
and fall.
I follow your breath
up those stairs.

The tarnished silver bell calls.
The tray trembles
as I bring breakfast
then lunch
up those same steps.
In between I climb to check:
still sleeping?
still breathing?

I follow your breath
everywhere I go.

TWENTY TWENTY

My husband apologized
to me today
for looking old.
"After 40 years of marriage,"
I countered,
"what am I?
Some kind of trophy bride?"

Oh, Sweetheart,
keep the lights low,
forget to wear your glasses,
close your eyes when we kiss.
Sit across the room from me,
blink into the dim,
continue to tell me I'm beautiful
and I'll believe,
will in turn take off my glasses
to see you as you were,
only better.
What a couple we are.
You and Me.

THE MAN IN THE HOTEL LUTETIA

We sit across the table
in the art deco piano bar
on the Left Bank
after a lifetime together
as if on our first date
while he charms me
with stories I've never heard
of when, a student,
he'd roomed right up the street
in a baroness's down-sized
furniture-crammed quarters
dependent on Americans like him—
We could have just met
the way he talks for me
flatters and intrigues me
sweeps me off my feet
like my girlhood matinee crushes
whisking me off in their arms. . .

Time to go
he stumbles slightly.
Permanently bent over
he reaches for his cane
needs my arm.
I offer it,
sympathetic but somehow removed
like a humane stranger
viewing an old man
across the street.
He needs my help,
poor old man.

A LOVE AFFAIR

You were white in your nightgown
white against the room's dark
as you called me in to say goodnight
your hair, long and tumbly
loose around your face
a face I tried to see mine in
my daughter in
but we two were left out
you were you
distinct, lovely
heartbreaking young
my granddaughter.

Will you ever again
love me as you did that night?
If so will you tell me?
The way you did then?
I still hear your voice
its lilt
its embrace:
"My wonn-derful, wonn-derful grandmother."
In love.
We were in love.

INSOMNIA

My husband…
I watch him breathe,
asleep
only asleep.
I will his heart to keep pumping
his lungs to keep working,
hoping I will never have to muzzle
his dear mouth with my breath,
never have to press his ribs
to startle and awaken his heart, my heart.
With no one else
am I totally me.
Alone, what?
I don't choose to know.
Don't leave.
Don't go.

MARTHA DEBORAH HALL

HIDDEN EMPTIES

No one joins me to watch "Meet the Press"
nor to carve the pot roast on Sunday nights.
Your "Sail" subscription finally lapsed.
Your alumni magazine arrived,
(I'll have to inform them.)

Each day our golden waits by the door
listening for your car to pull up.
I filled your half of the closet
with my winter clothes
and took one pillow off our bed.

Tractor keys rust on a hook in the barn.
I raked your empties from the hay in the stable.
The support boards from the saw horses
are not where you kicked them to the floor.
The dangling rope is gone.

JANICE H. MIKESELL

HURRICANE

she was there to see it, and
I need to believe her
the sea, the wind, the debris
the glass, the roofs, the turmoil

but after that
a bumper crop of babies
a sudden greening
everything bursting, bursting into bloom
tenacious
and out of season

how I long for a second blooming
arms around me, lips
man gripped between my thighs
husband's dementia—gone
daughter's hurts—resolved

just one last night of
bodies touching
and after that
a graceful drift
into oblivion

BOTANICAL GARDENS

late again
forgot again
promised
yes, promised
home early, noon concert
Botanical Gardens

I'll show him
take off
on my own
buy stuff
yeah, stuff
come home late
let him worry
for a change

front door opens
face beams with
Sunday morning smile, and
after-church righteousness
blue shirt, red tie, green tissue
enclosing
one scarlet rose

I wanted to do this
for you, he says
note enclosed:
I love it when
we're together

but…
the concert…

stricken…
I'm sorry, I'm sorry
I forgot

ashamed, I leap
and plant
a major kissy-face
a very major
kissy-face

and fall in love
with the same
damn man
for the one
thousandth time

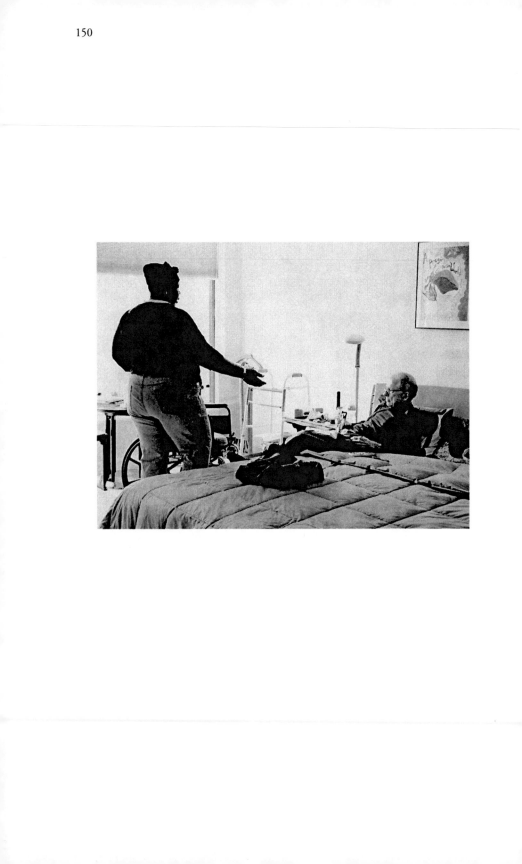

ANN GOETHE

COACH

His full name is James Allen Jackson, but no one has ever called him anything, but Coach. Shortly after we got married he took the job here at the college. In our first year the wrestling team gave him a purple satin jacket with 'Coach' written across the back. When it got too worn or stained, they would give him another one. Our son Jim was born and raised in this small town and when he decided to go far away for college, we supported his decision. After that, the house seemed empty, so Coach and I got two Pomeranians: Trixie and Tinker. He loved walking them around the neighborhood. It would make you smile to see that giant broad-shouldered man lumbering after those prissy little dogs. When he retired, the team gave us matching purple jackets. There were jokes about me 'coaching' Coach, and we all had a good laugh. Then, there we were, in our identical jackets, walking our sassy little dogs. Retirement suited us. We are both shy people, so didn't mind keeping to ourselves, taking care of the yard and following our own easy routines. Trixie died first, some type of kidney failure. It was like Coach went into mourning, he couldn't mention Trixie's name without tearing up. One afternoon he took Tinker off for a walk and didn't come back home until after dark. He said he'd forgotten the way. Almost fifty years in this town on this street and he couldn't find his way home. Talking about it, you could tell he was afraid of himself, his eyes cloudy and trapped looking at the same time. In the following year we lost Tinker and lost much of Coach too. He was so big and so disoriented; there were times it was dangerous to be by myself with him. Jim paid for 'companions' for Coach, strong young people to help me dress him, feed him and calm him when his lost feelings made him violent. Lately, all that rage seems gone. We had a hard winter, but now the first signs of spring are appearing. I've been leading Coach by the hand up and down our street pointing out the crocuses and snowdrops. It's just the two of us again, in our matching satin jackets, walking real slow.

PHIL RICHARDSON

LONDON BRIDGE IS FALLING DOWN

"You're just a fountain of information. Maybe we should get you a job as a guide while we're here."

Jeanne smiled at him, patted his hand, and returned to reading her guidebook. Martin looked at her and thought how lucky he was to spend his retirement with a wife like Jeanne. They had been married thirty years now, and he couldn't be happier.

His thoughts were interrupted when the guide picked up her microphone and began talking to the group about their arrival at the hotel. "Your bags will be taken to your rooms. You don't need to check in. Just get your keys and go directly to your rooms."

"They really make it simple," Jeanne said. "I love not having to lug those bags around."

Martin didn't reply, but chuckled inwardly. Jeanne never carried her own bags. She left that to him, no matter how many bags there were.

When they arrived at the hotel, there were the usual delays in getting off the bus as people got their things from the overhead racks. A smiling man clad in red livery, held the door of the hotel open for them and they entered the lobby. After a short wait in line, they got their room keys, took the elevator to their floor, and began what turned out to be a long journey to their room. A left turn, a right turn, down a long hall, up some steps, another turn and then another long corridor before they finally came to their room. Because it was a corner room, they had five windows and so it seemed light and airy. The furnishings were very much like what you would find in any American hotel except that the pictures on the wall were very tasteful. Their windows looked down on a lovely courtyard with a fountain and, since they were only on the third story, they could even hear the fountain splashing.

"Wonderful! Just look at the view!" Jeanne was ecstatic. "This is the nicest room we've ever had. Well, maybe the room in Pittsburgh was this good."

This puzzled Martin as he and Jeanne had never been to Pittsburgh, but he didn't say anything. Sometimes lately Jeanne got a little confused, but that was one of the things that endeared her to him. He started unpacking his clothes, as did Jeanne. She took the top drawer of the dresser—she always did, and he took the bottom one—he always did. They decided it was time for a nap after the long journey, so they slept until it was time to go to the evening reception. After another long traipse down the hallways and a ride on the elevator, they arrived at the Taj room where the reception was being held.

Jeanne was soon talking to a group of people as though she had known them all her life. Martin watched her from a quiet corner and thought how beautiful she was at age sixty. He looked down at his own paunch and, once more, decided to lose weight. Sighing at the thought of exercise, he motioned for the waiter to bring him another beer.

As he was sipping his beer and munching on an hors d'ouevre, Jeanne came over to him. "I was just talking to those nice people from New York, and they have a golden retriever like Bear. Do you have any pictures on you?"

"No, they're with those other pictures on top of the dresser in our room."

"Well, I do want to show them our dog. I'll go get them."

"I'll do it." He didn't really want to go all the way back to the room, but he made the gesture. Jeanne insisted, however, and, after making sure she had her key, she left. Martin began to get worried when she didn't come back after twenty minutes. Probably had to go to the bathroom, he thought. After ten more minutes, he went looking. She wasn't in the room. He went up to the next floor and then to the floor below. Finally he went to the lobby and there she was sitting on one of the sofas.

"What happened, Dear? Why didn't you come back to the reception room?"

Jeanne stood up and he could see tears in her eyes. "I couldn't find it. I couldn't find our room either. I thought if I came down here you would find me, and you did. I was too embarrassed to ask the desk clerk where my room was."

Jeanne had always had a bad sense of direction, so Martin chuckled and said, "Well, Dear, maybe I'll just have to put little markers on the hallways so you can find your way the next time. I could take a hatchet and blaze a trail like the Indians did."

Jeanne smiled at this and hurriedly wiped the tears from her eyes. "Always the smart aleck. My mother told me not to marry a smart aleck, but I got you anyway."

They went down the corridor to the elevator and up to their floor. Martin noticed that Jeanne was always making a wrong turn and realized that she really couldn't find her way to the room. With all the twists and turns and her bad sense of direction, he thought he understood this.

The next morning after a great English breakfast of bangers, eggs, stewed mushrooms, fruit and biscuits, they talked about the plan for the day. They had signed up for a Literary Tour of London, but it had been cancelled because not enough people wanted to walk around in the rain.

"Maybe we should go find that big Ferris wheel we saw from the bus," Jeanne suggested. "I've always liked Ferris wheels."

"The Eye of London is a little bit more than a Ferris wheel. It's so big that each of the cars is the size of a small bus."

"I think it would be fun, and it's raining, so we don't want to walk around too much."

"Anything you want to do is OK with me," Martin said. "I heard that the lines are very long, however."

Jeanne, as always, got her way and they walked from their hotel until they arrived at the bridge that would take them across the Thames to the Eye of London. It was still a good distance away, but it towered over all the other buildings.

"It must be at least twenty stories high," Martin said. "It doesn't seem to stop. I wonder how they get the passengers on and off? Are you sure you want to do this?"

Martin wouldn't admit it to Jeanne, but he had a fear of heights and he also wasn't convinced that the English were very good at maintenance. Nonetheless they bought their tickets and stood in line for almost an hour. Just before they boarded, however, the big wheel came to a stop. There was a lot of activity by the maintenance staff and Martin became concerned. He was wondering how those people felt who were at the top of the wheel, stuck there until someone got the thing going again. Jeanne didn't seem to care, however, and was upset with the delay.

"This would never happen back home," she said. "The lines aren't so long there either."

"Back home? What do you mean? We don't have a Ferris wheel in Hillsdale."

"Oh, you know, at the county fair."

There hadn't been a county fair in Hillsdale for twenty years, but Martin said nothing.

Just then the big wheel began moving again and so did the line. Soon they had boarded the Eye of London car—the process was tricky, as they had to walk along and, more or less, match the speed of the moving car and then quickly board it. It took half-an-hour for the car to make the circuit and Martin spent most of the time sitting on a bench in the middle of the car so he wouldn't feel the height so much. Jeanne took a lot of pictures of Big Ben, the Thames, and the Parliament buildings. It seemed strange that they were as far above all the buildings as if they were riding in a helicopter.

When they finally exited their car, a tricky proposition, which was the reversal of the boarding process, Jeanne said she was too tired to walk back to the hotel so they took a cab. Instead of going to their room, however, Martin decided that he needed a beer to overcome the queasy stomach he had developed on the ride. They walked the half-block to Albert's Pub, and he ordered a pint of Guinness for himself and a gin and tonic for Jeanne. When he got back to the table, however, she was gone. Her purse was lying on the table and her raincoat was folded over the back of the chair, but no Jeanne in sight.

I wonder where she's off to now, Martin thought. She just can't seem to sit still very long these days. Glancing around, he finally spotted her talking to a couple at another table.

"Jeanne," he called. "Here's your drink. Come and sit down."

The couple seemed relieved when she left and Martin wondered what she had been saying to them. Jeanne sat down and sipped at her drink. She seemed distracted, so Martin began discussing their plans for the next day.

He wanted to go to the Imperial War Museum. Jeanne wasn't too thrilled with the idea, however.

"Dusty old guns and tanks and airplanes. Why don't you just read a book about them instead? I think I'll go to the Tate Museum and get some real culture."

"Dusty old paintings and statues," Martin kidded. "Why don't you just get a book and read about them?"

They laughed together and decided to do their own thing for the morning and then meet at lunch.

The next morning, over breakfast, Martin suggested that they go over the subway and street plan so Jeanne wouldn't get lost in London's twists and turns. He marked the underground stops and circled the hotel's location on the map.

"Just remember Jeanne," he said. "If you get lost there are lots of Bobbies about and they can give you directions."

"I won't get lost, Dear. I have your map, and I can always flag down one of those wonderful London cabs to bring me back to the hotel."

Mollified by this, Martin left for his morning in the War Museum. It was everything he wanted—lots of tanks, guns, airplanes, and even a "blitz experience" where you sat in a fake cellar and listened to fake bombs falling. He was so engrossed that it was almost lunchtime when he left, and he had to take a cab back to the hotel. Jeanne hadn't arrived, however, and he went to the room to wait. Feeling just a little bit of jet lag, he decided to take a nap until Jeanne returned.

It was almost two hours later when he awakened. At first he didn't know where he was, but then he sat up and looked once more at his watch. Jeanne should have been back by now. There was no message light blinking on the telephone, but he called the desk just in case.

"No messages for your room," the operator's voice replied, "just check the light on your telephone to see if there are any messages."

Martin hung up, slightly peeved with the operator's mild rebuke. Jeanne probably got lost, he thought. Lord knows I've been lost enough times in London with all those twisty, curvy, streets. After stretching a bit, he put on his coat and went to the lobby to wait.

By three o'clock he was beginning to worry. He decided to go to the information room and see if their tour group leader could give him some advice on what to do.

"Your wife just probably got a little bit disoriented," Bob, the tour group leader told him. "I've had people disappear for hours because they took the wrong bus or tube."

Martin finally convinced Bob that Jeanne had been gone too long for just getting lost and asked him to contact the police. Bob was reluctant, but he finally called. After a brief conversation with the police, Bob told Martin there was no news, but the police would call the hotel if she were to show up.

"What are they doing? Are they really looking for her or are they just doing like they would in the States, nothing?"

"They'll call. This is London, you know. If anyone shows up at a police station or in the hospital, they'll call."

Frustrated, Martin couldn't decide what to do. Finally, he went to the front desk, alerted them to the fact that his wife was missing and then went to the room.

For the next several hours he paced the floor and then he stood in front of the phone, willing it to ring. He wanted to hear Jeanne say, "Darling, I got lost. I'm taking a cab, and I'll be there soon."

By 8 p.m. Martin was a nervous wreck. He had resisted the temptation to loot the minibar and get drunk because he wanted to be able to deal with whatever situation arose. He called the front desk again, but they had heard nothing. Jeanne knew they had tickets (very hard to get) to "Phantom of the Opera" and now they had missed it. She would have made it back in time if she could. Martin imagined her lying on a hospital bed or in a morgue. Something bad had to have happened or she would be here.

It was almost midnight when his phone rang. It was the front desk calling to tell him that a policeman wished to see him. Not waiting to ask why, he rushed out the door, ran down the twisting corridors and, when he arrived at the elevator he slammed his palm against the down button as if the energy of his hammering would bring the car faster. When the doors opened, he rushed into the car and, unable to stand still, paced back and forth until it arrived at the lobby level. He ran to the front desk and almost fainted with relief when he saw Jeanne standing there with a policeman.

"Jeanne! Jeanne! You're all right! Thank God!" He grabbed her in his arms and hugged her as tight as he could. Then he turned to the policeman. "Thank you, thank you for bringing her back to me."

"Found her standing in the middle of the street down by the Thames walkway, Sir. She was obviously lost, and we had a report to look out for an American woman, so I stopped."

"That's wonderful," Martin said. "I guess I'm surprised she didn't take a cab back."

Jeanne looked a little strange when Tom said this. "I...I couldn't remember the name of the hotel," she said.

"Sir, could I speak to you privately?" The policeman motioned for Martin to join him as he moved away from Jeanne.

Martin followed him over to a corner and then listened in horror as the policeman told him that Jeanne had not known her name. She had given the name "Jeanne Hardy" when asked and, of course, Martin knew that was her maiden name. He couldn't understand how she could have done this. He could understand how she could have gotten lost, but not knowing her married name; that was something else. After signing the policeman's report, Martin thanked him again and returned to Jeanne.

"I'm so sorry," she said as they walked to their room. "London is so big. I left my purse someplace, and I didn't have any money, and I didn't have my glasses, and I didn't know where you were."

"It's all right." Martin took her hand as they walked down the hallway. "I guess the big city is just too much for you alone. I think we should cut the tour short and go home tomorrow."

"Home would be nice," she replied. "The streets are straight and there are no bridges. I remember now that I was walking across a big bridge just before I got lost."

"Yes, dear, London Bridge."

"Mother used to sing me that song," she said and then her voice changed to a higher pitch as she sang softly, "London Bridge is falling down, falling down...I, I can't remember the rest. Funny, I liked it so much."

She stopped walking, turned to him, and smiled. "Daddy, would you sing it to me, before I go to bed?"

REGINA MURRAY BRAULT

THE LAST PAGE

When Annie's bones could no longer
hold her body erect,
Walter carried their bed downstairs
near the window that overlooked the brook,
then slipped her softly between the sheets.
He opened Volume A of their encyclopedias
and they talked about aardvarks,
he leading the way with text,
she was whispering questions,
both pausing to watch the red fox
quenching his thirst at sundown.
After each day's reading, Walter carefully folded
the corner of the page—all the way to dragonfly.

FRANK SALVIDIO

SHADOWLAND

If I should slip into the shadows of
Your mind, there to become a living ghost,
Half-seen, mistaken for some other love,
Some other friend, my face forgotten, lost
Upon a sea of shapes, a distant ship
Obscured in mist and fog, my voice unheard
Or poised in breath upon another's lip,
A whisper that will not become a word:
In this confusion, can my memory
Of us survive if I do not survive
In you—if you can neither hear nor see
The common memory that keeps us alive?
If our two memories are lived as one,
How can both live when one of them is done?

NOW

I know there was a time before your time,
But I do not remember it; do not
Recall when music, movie, book or rhyme
Did not involve your mind in mine, nor art
Impress without your knowing nod; your word
Not make the ancient apologue seem new,
The long-accepted narrative absurd,
Not separate the bogus from the true.
And if no longer lovers now, what are
We then, so intimately bound in thought
We think each in the other's mind, who were
But bodies once and only passion sought?
Say, two turbulent streams—met suddenly—
Conjoined to one to run on tranquilly.

AFTER RADIATION

The times have found me out at last, and bare
Necessity has taken me in hand,
And of my manhood made me unaware—
Unfeatured, disconnected, dry as sand—
Yet still alive to every mortal urge
Of wanton memory no errant ray
Can quite efface, no random ion purge,
Whatever of myself is burned away.
And though I cannot stir, by wish or will,
Spent nerves addressed in vain, cannot renew
Lost moments that recall of rapture still,
Yet I delight my soul in loving you,
Not to relive, but to record, what's past:
No matter where I loved, I loved you last.

HER FACE

I thought that it was love merely to sigh
And sing, to fashion measured lines in praise
Of her "fair face"—to magnify her eye
Or gloss her lip in ballads, sonnets, lays—
To make a compost heap of words and call
It poetry, not so to praise her name
Or nurture images that would recall
Her face as to achieve a poet's fame.
But now that Time has made that face so plain
No memory of it—no poet's art—
Can give it back that loveliness again
That once it had, that moved my pen and heart
To flatter what I have seen Time remove,
Yet long to see no other—that is love.

PHYLLIS LANGTON

WAITING
—Dedicated to Gentleman George

It is October of 2000, and George's appointment with the neurologist falls on Friday the 13th. On that ominous date, we sit in the neurologist's office as he tells us the news. "George," he says, "I think you have a motor neuron disease, ALS, commonly referred to as Lou Gehrig's disease. It causes rapid deterioration of voluntary muscle activity. You probably have six months to live. Go out and have a good time; do all the fun things you've wanted to do and haven't done, while you can still do them. The only treatment is a drug, Rilutek, which may extend your life another month, though it does have potential side effects, such as liver and kidney damage. Before you start it, I need to do multiple tests and extensive blood work. You should consider the drug. Come back and see me in a week."

I am devastated. I drop my purse on the floor when George answers him. "You tell me I have six months to live, but if I take a drug that involves more tests and possible liver damage, I may live another month or two, with a lousy quality of life. What the hell nonsense is that? My liver is working just fine, and it will stay that way until I die. I see no reason to return. Thank you."

George stand ups and prepares to leave. I watch his face and can see his lips drawn tight in a thin line that I recognize as controlled anger. His pupils are fixed. I know he has shut down and isn't going to listen, or negotiate anything. I hold his arm as we leave the office.

He has just been given a death sentence, and I am scared he might fall on the way to the car. He has been falling more often lately. When we approach the car he says, "Well, I guess I know what's going to be on my death certificate. That's more than you can say." He pats my arm as if to reassure me. With the wit, courage, and strength of that moment, he sets the tone for the journey we will travel.

It is now October 2002, two years later. The wicked disease is relentlessly devouring his body, eating its way through arm and leg muscles, and making its way toward the diaphragm muscle he must use to breathe. Just when his body adjusts to one change, without warning, he falls to another plateau.

And yet George is brave. He is also stoic, and gentlemanly, having been born in the 1920s in a polite community in New Jersey at a time when children hid their feelings and were to be seen and not heard. As for me, I am strong too, but I'm a scrappy fighter, with noisy, impish tendencies—a graduate of a Boston orphanage where I was dumped in the Great Depression of the early 1930s.

But while we are polar opposites on the surface, under the skin we're the same. We always manage to work through any disagreements, such as when he is cranky and stubborn when I use the handicapped parking spaces. He tells me to park some other place, or he'll stay in the car. He doesn't want to be viewed as a "cripple."

I try tough love, saying that he can sit in the car and enjoy his stubbornness if he doesn't want to help me with the necessary errands, or get out to enjoy the first sunny day in two weeks. Then I add, "There's nothing to be embarrassed about. You have this lousy disease and unfortunately you're dying, but you're just human." As I start to get out of the car he mutters, "OK, woman, get me out of here."

I reach over and hug him, run to the back of the car and pull out the lightweight leather transport wheelchair that I can throw in the back of the car when he has to walk any distance, or in the house when he is tired. After two severe falls, I insist we use the wheelchair in public. This is our compromise, as he objects to a heavy, battery-operated wheelchair that he sees as useless; he can't control his lifeless arms and fingers.

After dinner one evening in July, after we have finished watching the Wimbledon tennis finals in the family room, he is especially quiet. Tennis was always such an important part of our lives together and with our friends. We are feeling a little weepy as we joke about the fact that I still play for him in his men's groups, using his god-awful heavy racket, so that he is still "on the court" with his buddies. He watches from the balcony of the indoor tennis facility, and his friends tease him at dinner, telling him I am prettier and faster than he. On the way home he remarks how different the game looks when he's sitting on the bench, as he coaches me on their playing strategies.

As I finish cleaning up the kitchen, I ask him to tell me about some of his greatest frustrations so far during this journey. He doesn't answer. I wonder if he's heard me since he doesn't wear his hearing aid anymore. Or perhaps he's gone to sleep.

Finally, he says, "I'm tired of waiting."

"Waiting? For what?" I ask.

"That could take all night. There's just too much to say."

"Well, I have all night. Let's talk about it."

I prepare him a hot toddy with his favorite Bushmills Irish whiskey, which is his only pain medicine, and a glass of pinot noir wine for me. I lift him from the wheelchair, tuck him into his favorite black leather chair, and cover his legs with a light, summer blanket, as his legs get cold and painful now when he sits for more than an hour. I place his drink on the cherry end table next to his chair so he can bend down and sip it from a long glass straw, without my help. I know this pleases him because he winks at me as he sips his drink.

We talk for more than an hour, with our eyes tearing up in pain and tender laughter. It is the first time he shares what it means to him to wait for each moment of living—and dying. George says:

"When I wake up, I wait to see if my eyes are getting worse and if I can move my head, arms, or legs. My eyes don't focus like they used to, and each day I can move less. I look back six months, three months and see what I have lost.

"I wait to see if I can still whistle. I worry that I won't be able to call you when I need you, if I lose my whistle. We joke that this is the only time I can get away with whistling for you without getting a shoe thrown at me.

"I wait for your smile.

"I wait for you to get me out of bed into the wheelchair; lift me out of the wheelchair onto the bidet; and then close the bathroom door and let me sit a few minutes, alone for a few minutes. You tell me it it's time for bowel movements with Beethoven, as you turn on the Bose music system. You add that you would love to smell some sweet-smelling shit when you come back. You tease me and tell me there are no bowel movements in heaven and that's why all you men want to go there.

"I wait for you to get me back into my wheelchair, wash my hands and face, comb my hair, and take me downstairs.

"I wait for you to turn on the news and feed me my favorite breakfast of old-fashioned oatmeal, orange juice, toast, and strong coffee. And I watch the news while you clean up the kitchen.

"I wait for you to take me upstairs after breakfast and prepare me for my shower, undress me and lift me from the wheelchair onto the shower chair, all the time talking to me—hugging and holding me. I tell you, 'Hurry up, woman. I don't have all day.' And then I say, 'Hey, slow down, woman, this is kinda fun—just like our honeymoon.' We play like the new baby Chinese pandas at the Washington Zoo.

"I wait for you to rub shampoo on my head, massage my scalp as you wash my hair. Then you run the shower water over my body and let me relax with the warm water running over my back and legs. That feels so good. You seem to get wetter than I do, so I tell you to wear your bikini the next time, or maybe nothing. Then you call me a randy old fighter pilot, and smack me on my disappearing butt.

"I wait for you to dry me and dress me after I tell you what I want to wear. You sit on the floor and struggle to put on my socks and shoes because I can't push with my feet, or hold my feet or legs up to help you. But you won't let me wear slippers during the day and feel like a prisoner of war, deprived of the dignity of socks and shoes.

"I wait while you rub talcum powder on my face before you use my electric razor to shave off the stubble on my chin. I watch you in the mirror and see my facial structure is melting away. Sometimes I tease you when you brush my teeth with the electric toothbrush as I nibble on your fingers. We always laugh a lot.

"I wait while you get me seated in front of my computer, which you help me use, because my hands aren't agile enough. We're a funny looking pair. You don't know how to work the computer. And I know how, but I can't because my hands don't work any more.

"I wait for you to turn on the TV station that carries the investment news. I know that soon I won't be able to manage our investment portfolio, so I need to teach you. You tell me you don't have time to learn about investing money, and that worries me.

"I wait for our grandchildren to visit, climb up in my bed, sit all over me, wash my face, and feed me lunch, chattering all the time. They are so excited that sometimes they push the food in my mouth so fast their spoons hit each other and the food falls out. You have to slow them down before I start to choke, which happens more often now. I love to hear them tell me, 'Grandpa George, you can't go out and play unless you eat all your lunch.' Then you get me out of bed so the girls can walk me around the room using the wobbly crutches they've made for me with tiny pieces of wooden tinker toys. You grab me hard from behind by my sweat pants to hold me up, and I tell you, 'Careful woman, you are maiming my manhood.' The girls place a crutch under each arm, hold my hands and we parade to the elevator. I clench my teeth and suck in my breath to concentrate on standing tall.

"I wait for Joy, our hospice nurse, and Dr. Hank, to come for their visits. I tell Joy, "Ain't got no satisfaction. Ain't had no bowel action.' They do their usual examinations and listen to my chest for noises that show I might be retaining fluids in my lungs. I'm exhausted after they leave. It's hard to be up for visits and examinations when you're worn out from any effort at all.

"I wait for people who visit to say something other than, 'And how are you feeling today, George?' I want to say to them, 'How the hell do you think I'm feeling? I have Lou Gehrig's disease, and I'm going to die soon. How would you feel?'

"I wait for the home health aide to stay with me while you go to the university to teach, since I can't be left alone anymore. And I wait for the sound of the garage door at the end of the day, because I know it's you getting home. I wait for you to fix my hot toddy and our dinner, feed me, and tell me all the news about your classes and university politics.

"I wait for our nights out to the Old Brogue Pub for an evening of fun with my buddies and enjoying some Bushmills Irish whiskey. I tease you when you have to slide me in and out of the car using a forty-gallon plastic trash bag.

"I wait for you to take me upstairs to prepare me for bed. The evening ritual is exhausting as you undress me, seat me on the bidet, later dress me in my pajamas, brush my teeth, get me into bed, rub and kiss my forehead, and tell me to stay there. Sometimes I forget, and you have to scoop me off the floor to put me back into bed, or call the neighbors, or the fire department for help. Finally, you tell me you have ordered a hospital bed with side rails to keep me in bed when I forget. I'm not happy with this idea. But you say, 'You have your choice: either a hospital bed, or the scroungiest-nursing home I can find, and I've found two already.'

"I'm always waiting for something to happen to me, or to be done to me. Time hangs on, and the loneliness creeps in— haunting me.

"I wait and watch myself die a little every day. It's probably hard for you to imagine the searing exhaustion I go through. I can't do anything for myself. 'Well,' you tell me, 'you can still breath without any difficulty. So get off the pity pot.'

"I wait for sleep because that's the only time I feel better."

I am sitting by his bed the next morning when he awakens. I watch his eyes search the room until they land on my face, as I smile at him. "Hey, there," I say, holding in my hand a ribbon attached to some jingle bells. "I am going to tie these bells around your wrist so that if you lose your whistle, you can shake your bells."

He laughs and says, "Phyllis you are the craziest person I know."

I think, "What a benefit to be crazy in this situation."

Over breakfast, we talk about how we can help each other work through all the monotonous, lonely moments.

I say, "I have made a list of your buddies. Each day, you select one, and I'll put you on the speakerphone so you can talk with him. I know you don't think the telephone is the best way to communicate, and you think us women talk too much. Perhaps we do, but that's because we care about each other, and aren't afraid to show it. There are no secrets among friends who care. Your buddies care about you and want to talk to you, not me. You need to reach out and do this. Are you willing to try?"

"We can try it," he answers. "I know better than to fight with you because you are going to do it anyway, so okay."

I continue, "Next, since I need to learn investment strategies, you can teach me the principles of handling a portfolio. You've taught this before many times at the university and your lecture notes aren't completely yellowed. And your brain is still alert. You can teach it again. I'll be your assistant and you can dictate your revised lecture notes to me. How does that sound?"

The old familiar smile returns to his face, which seems to bring color back to his cheeks. He sits straight up in the bed and says, "Have you been up all night planning this?"

"Of course." I answer.

And so we go on, waiting together.

CELEBRATING LIFE IS FOREVER

Dear Gentleman George,

On March 20, 2003, at 3:15 a.m., you die peacefully at home after you talk to me while I hold your hand. I have no energy to move. I sit by your side and revisit some of the memories we built during these last three years of your struggles with Lou Gehrig's disease. The ceiling fan whirls above my head. The only sound I hear is the heater as it cycles. Life has left the house.

I feel chilled and run the bath water especially hot. I crave all the bubbles and the sweet scent of lavender. I sink into the tub and weep.

After a while, in a daze, I remember that I have to call the hospice nurse to come and pronounce you dead, and the transport service to take you to the funeral home in Arlington, Virginia. I decide to let them both sleep longer.

A few hours later, the hospice nurse certifies your death, and the pickup service prepares to transport your body to the funeral home. The vehicle carrying your body pulls out of our driveway at 7:00 a.m. I follow it to the funeral home and hope I have brought all the necessary documents.

A gray-haired man wearing a black, pinstriped suit meets me at the door with a broad smile and a firm handshake, despite his gnarled, arthritic knuckles and twisted fingers. He is tall and thin like a skeleton, with protruding, brown eyes. He shuffles his feet, making a whish sound. I wonder if I have awakened him.

After we introduce ourselves, we sit down with me opposite him at his highly polished, wooden desk, covered with piles of booklets, leaflets, and forms. I wonder how long this exchange will take and how much it will cost. My experience with funeral directors has been rare, and my friends have warned me to be alert for the pressures of this business: helping vulnerable people spend large amounts of money.

He begins with his list of questions: where will Dr. Thomas be buried; what memorial services are to be held, and where; what visiting hours do I want for viewing of the deceased; and other questions that develop from my responses.

After I tell him that you were a veteran of World War II, Korea, and Vietnam and a highly decorated fighter pilot, his face brightens, and he puffs his chest to an amazing size for a skeleton.

"As a veteran, he is entitled to be buried in Arlington Cemetery. That takes some time to schedule, probably four to five months. But we can help you with that."

"Thank you, but he doesn't wish to be buried in Arlington Cemetery."

You can hear the silence as he stares at me.

"I don't understand," he says.

"There's nothing to understand. He wants to be cremated and have his ashes scattered."

"Oh, that's fine. His urn can be placed in the Tomb, a special section of the cemetery. Many people do that today. That requires scheduling, also. Now what about viewing hours here at our chapel?"

"No viewing hours. He wants his friends to remember him as he was when he was alive, not dead and made up with whatever stuff you put in bodies, or on them."

"Do you want to have a memorial service here first with his casket closed?" he asks.

"No. He doesn't want a memorial or a funeral service. He wants a big party for his family and friends to celebrate his life by dancing to New Orleans jazz music played by the Professors; and he wants them to drink good beer, wine and Irish whiskey at his favorite inn in Upperville, Virginia."

The silence is palpable. I can see sweat on his forehead. He is shuffling his feet under the desk. I haven't agreed to any of his options and we have been talking for over thirty minutes. I see the look on his face shift from smiles and charm to solemn, matter-of-fact business.

I break the silence. "I would like him cremated in one of your usual cremation containers, and I'd like to pick up his ashes when they are ready. Also, as his widow, I am entitled to have his flag, even if he isn't buried in Arlington Cemetery."

He looks at me with a wide-open stare. "You want his flag?"

"Yes."

He lowers his head and picks up a form for me to sign with a list of charges and associated costs. I agree to the fees, and ask him to get my flag, while I tell you goodbye.

He presses a bell under his desk, and a heavyset young man with bursting pimples on his face tells me to follow him. Lying on the narrow stretcher, you appear lifelike and peaceful, and as neat as a soldier, still wearing your pale blue pajamas, with every gray hair in place. Your eyes and mouth are firmly closed. I rub and kiss your forehead, which you liked me to do when I kissed you goodnight, after tucking you into bed.

"Goodbye, Mr. Blue Eyes. Rest your arms in peace, my love. I am going home to plan your celebration of life party. I won't forget to tell everyone what you said: 'Don't let anyone get up and say what a great guy I am, or it may start a fight. Dance, drink lots of good Irish whiskey, and eat plenty of food, because I'm paying for this.'"

I return to the front area, pick up your flag, write a check for the funeral home's services, and make an appointment to return for your ashes the following Monday.

On Sunday, April 27, 2003, at 11:00 a.m., I arrive with my cousins at the 1763 Inn in Upperville, Virginia, to complete the preparations for your farewell party, which begins at noon. It is like coming home as I breathe in the fresh air blowing off the peaks of the Shenandoah and Blue Ridge Mountains. The log cabins still cover part of the thirty-three acres. The many sections of pasture—separated by black, wooden, horse fences—are still home to many horses and cattle. The bright sun shimmers on the lake at the bottom of the hill below the Inn. I think of how many times during the last five years we fed the three ducks there—the ones supervised by that bossy, aristocratic swan sitting on her ferociously guarded tennis balls.

My cousins and I unload the car and place twelve over-sized poster boards depicting your life story in the Inn's open cabana. The poster boards begin with a picture of you and your parents at the New Jersey Shore, when you were fourteen months. You look like you were dancing across the sand as your parents hung onto your little hands. Even at that age, you were smiling.

Other posters show you in your New Jersey National Guard uniform; in your Army Air Corps uniform in World War II; and at your graduation from West Point in 1948. There are also pictures of you with your airplanes during the Korean and Vietnam Wars, and pictures of us with our family and friends.

I find our hostess, Uta, and review the sumptuous brunch menu you selected for your party: corned beef and cabbage, sauerbraten, knockwurst, red cabbage, coleslaw, pickled beets, your favorite green beans, baked salmon, a variety of omelets and breads, salads, Irish whiskey cake, and sandwiches and snacks for the many children. There is something for everyone.

I am expecting 160 friends and family for the party, coming from as far as California, Florida, Ohio, and other distant places, who will stay in some of the log cabins. I want to make sure everything is in place. I begin a last-minute check of the bar, set up with wine, beer, and Bushmills Irish whiskey; and the location of the podium and microphone for people who may want to tell stories about you. I check the tables inside and outside the cabana for flowers, a copy of my tribute to you, and lyrics of "When the Saints Come Marching In," which we will sing as we send you on your new journey.

I look up and see the Professors, from Shenandoah University, elegant and smart in their tuxedos, approaching the cabana with their instruments: trombone, clarinet, trumpet, violin, French horn, guitar, double bass, saxophones, and several percussion instruments. They have played for us before and are skillful at switching instruments, carrying us to new heights, or a shift in mood, depending upon the songs they are playing. We review the general program for break times, and when I will signal them for the grand finale.

I steal away for a few moments of quiet, taking some deep breaths to regain my strength because I feel pain in the pit of my stomach and like I will unravel soon. I stare at the sky, which is dotted with fair-weather, cumulus clouds, and remember the last party we had. It was October 2001, and we were celebrating your first year of life after you were diagnosed with Lou Gehrig's disease and were told you had six months to live. You said to me, "What a great day to fly. You want to fly with me, honey? This is a rehearsal for my real party to come." Today, I will be flying with you.

As our friends arrive, the Professors play a medley of World War II–era dance and jazz pieces—especially songs that Dizzie Gillespie and Louis Armstrong made popular. Soon, people are drinking, dancing, eating, milling around, hopping tables, and hugging, as we always do when we get together to celebrate. Many guests are also reading the poster boards illustrating your life. You are a humble, private man, and few people know of your many accomplishments in the Air Force, like two Distinguished Flying Crosses—a fighter pilot's most coveted decoration—and ten meritorious Air Medals.

As I scan the crowd, I think about how you chose to join the newly formed Air Force after graduating from West Point in 1948, even though most of your classmates joined the Army. And although you had little contact with these friends during most of your military career, they are all here today.

So many children are here, too, from little ones to teenagers. They eat like grazing cows, run around, and play hide and seek in the bright sun and cool breeze. Some dance with each other on the grass; others dance with their parents on the wooden dance floor in the cabana.

Now we gather, and people share stories about their friendship with you. One classmate tells of your adventures as a cadet, a horseman, and a polo player, explaining how you rode the mule at the noisy West Point football games. You used to say you were the jackass on top, and more stubborn than the mule. Others speak of your contributions as class treasurer and class president. And friends remember how, in later years, you helped teach wives and widows how to manage their financial affairs.

I share the story of how we first met on a blind date in 1970, as well as the funny tale you would tell of our decision to marry in 1987. You'd joke to our friends, "Phyllis called me in April and said, 'George, the answer is yes.' I asked her, 'What is the question?' She said, 'Yes, George, I will marry you.' 'Phyllis, I asked you to marry me seventeen years ago and you said no. I'll have to think about it. I'll call you back in two weeks.'" It was that over-the-top sense of humor that always kept us laughing.

The stories continue with our hospice nurse, Joy, who was with us for over a year. Joy explains how I would prepare a list of changes in your condition, as well as any unusual events since her last visit. She pulls a list out of her pocket, and reads, "George fell off the barstool." That causes so much laughter that she has difficulty finishing her stories.

Our dear neighbor, Larry, tells how a week before you died, he ran over in the middle of the night to lift you off the floor after you had climbed over the side rail of your hospital bed. He also shares how he helped me, after your death, figure out how to display your medals in the correct position and order on the poster boards. When he finishes speaking, he adds, "And

Phyllis, you put some of George's medals upside down." People roar with laughter as nearly six-foot, 170-pound Larry scoops me up in his arms for a great big hug and says, "Good job, Phyllis."

The laughter swells to great heights as our friends eat, drink, hug, and tell funny stories about you. Kids laugh in the background. At this point, I am overwhelmed and about to faint. I remember my yoga training and start breathing deeply so I can stay focused on the party.

I thank everyone for traveling this journey with us for three years; for coming to your first celebration of life party here in 2001; for coming to this final celebration of life party to send you off; and for many years of loving friendship.

We lift our glasses to you in friendship as I signal the Professors to play "Just a Closer Walk with Thee." Then we follow the Professors, who raise their horns to the sky, playing "When the Saints Go Marching In," as they parade out to the grass and pond. Music is in the air as we march from the cabana onto the grounds around the lake, with the swan hollering and honking with us. As we march, we sing with mixed voices, "Oh, when the saints go marching in, Oh, when the saints go marching in, Lord, how I want to be in that number, When the saints go marching in."

I feel jubilant that I am sending you off in the style you wanted, with the music you loved.

I return to the Inn a week later on our wedding anniversary to eat lunch with our friends, who created a memorial garden for you across the lake on the opposite hill. They offer to go with me to scatter your ashes. I thank them again for all their gracious support throughout this journey and tell them I want to have some quiet time with you now, after all the celebration has finished. Tears sting the corners of my eyes as we toast you with a glass of wine as we look across the lake to your garden.

I sit on the cedar bench in your garden and run my hands over the gold plaque that reads "Gentleman George." I tell you I have come to scatter your ashes in this special place. I gaze at the familiar swan on the lake, which is still sitting on her tennis balls.

I hold you on my lap in the cordovan, cardboard box that contains your cremains. The box is heavy and feels leathery and smooth. I open it, remove the twist tie from the clear plastic bag, and run my fingers through your crushed body that is now fine dust and cool, grayish-white powder. It gives off a musky odor. Grasping tiny fragments of your bones that made it through the fire and grinders, I think of the times I ran my hands, with tenderness and passion, over your muscled body. My eyes are full of salt and grime. I want to run away, to keep your ashes with me forever.

I feel the bile in my throat, as it tightens. It is hard to breathe, and a cold shiver runs up my back. My heart races as I stumble through the mass of weeds and plants, gently leaving parts of you everywhere, talking to you amidst my tears. You drift through my fingers like grains of sand.

Finally, I see shadows of sunlight on the front of your tombstone as I kneel on the grass to tell you goodbye. I pick up pieces of tangled grass that look like bean sprouts finding a new life. They are beginning again. It is spring.

> Goodbye, sweetie,
> Your loving wife, Phyllis

MOVING ON

ROGER B. SMITH

YES & NO

i am escorting a woman
who calls me
by another man's name
down into her dream

she hums gospel
i evoke god
i am excluded from both
but manage the rolling waves

after all
it's the 21st century
and she will
take palpitations as she can

& i will lie back
repeating my
new name
in pulsation

while rolling
away from her vacant
beauty
a game we play & play

REUNITED

most folks have some name for it
a stone in a favorite old shoe
at an inappropriate time

burrowing into soft flesh here you stand
i tried to pay attention when you told me
your life story

the road got rough
my stride shortened
before yours

the light got too familiar too
i was ready to sit down
at your entrance

DAHLIAS

i don't know what they look like any more

than paris or sweden or the cape of good hopes
still there is a love catalog around the house somewhere
full of pictures
of dahlias looking like bleached skeletons
& black mums silent against st augustine's
gray stucco walls of sea shells with cannon pocks

we've traveled hours & hours while reading
rimbaud elliott cummings
& sit through recitals
your hand in my trouser pocket
we find lyrics on the page
no matter where we happen to be

i wonder if this is real love
she said
as we sang the heady romantic part
a hand from nowhere
gently squeezing my crotch

the Spanish painter preferred mozart & vivaldi
but after all
that was beside the pacific
and this is not real love
only flowers

MARY O'DELL

BEING HERE, SUNDAY AFTERNOON

I could say
when I saw you my whole life ignited at once.

I could say *Oh* and *Ohh* and *Why did it take so long*
but none of those things would be true.

What's true is
when I saw you, a smile began in my middle

and crept out and out
until I was as comfortable as I've ever been.

When I saw you, I didn't regret the years
I didn't know you.

I was only glad that this is now
and you're in it.

When I saw you
I was as at home in my skin as you were in yours.

I don't know what to call this place
where our shadows merge.

I only know that being here
moves me easy, like breezes in the grass

restores me as sweetly as honeybees
romancing the clover.

THREE A.M., AND WAKING

I dream the sweet bulk of you
sleeping here
arm resting over my body

breath coming quiet, measured
the noise of your thoughts stilled for a time
as fatigue works its genial spell.

Some say giving over to sleep
in another's presence
implies greater closeness than heated caresses.

Sensing you only my hand's breadth away
I know this is true.
Weaving your fingers with mine

I nestle into the solid curve of your body
and breathe you in.
Drift on, love,

for peace can be hard to come by.
While you can,
share mine.

GARDEN TIME

My arms are old, he says,
plucking at the flesh above his elbow.

Her gaze drops to her own bare arms,
soft and pocked with age.

What a pair they are, here among the flowers
in their shorts and tee-shirts.

She lays her hand on his white thigh
and his smile lights the night.

He says, I love your morning glories,
those dark-leafed geraniums.

When his arms encircle her—
his old, pale arms—she lays her head against him

and listens to his heartbeat, slow and steady
as the rain soon coming to fall on the flowers.

BERNICE M. FISHER

THE ANONYMOUS ARTIST OF VICTORIA PARK

I was sixteen when I first heard the siren call of the Scarlett O'Hara house.

Alone on a bluff overlooking the Mississippi River, the house stood mute and kept its secrets, a silent witness to the barges and excursion boats churning up and down the river a few hundred feet away. Only the lace curtains fluttering in an open window hinted at the presence of life inside.

Progress had scorned the gaping maws of broken windows and the ruined grandeur of the houses in Victoria Park, a block away. Every summer, spears of emaciated daylilies reached up through gaps in sagging stairways, and every winter, squirrels ran across broken sidewalk stones and left spidery trails in the snow to mark their passage.

Four Ionic pillars stretched across the front of the white house, and a pair of topiaries stood as sentinels on each side of the carved front door. A broad expanse of manicured lawn erupted in a garden, where masses of flowers bloomed—scarlet cosmos, Asiatic lilies in white, pink and yellow, and red roses, their heavy perfume wafted toward us on the summer breezes. We called it the Scarlett O'Hara house, because it looked like one of those Southern mansions we saw in movies.

Who, I wondered, lived behind the white pillars? No one ever looked out a window or stood on the spindled balcony above the front door to wave, or walked across the yard to sit on the wrought iron bench near the garden.

I turn a corner on my first walk around Victoria Park, two days after I've moved into my new condo, and there it is, the white house, just as I remember it, with the shadows of oak trees sliding across the pillars. Lace curtains still grace the windows, but nothing remains of the garden's former splendor except some forlorn peony bushes waging a hopeless struggle for survival beneath a tangle of Virginia Creepers. I feel the ground tremble beneath my feet when a train rattles past, invisible below the sheer drop of a fifty-foot retaining wall a few yards away. Beyond, the Mississippi curves around a bend past downtown St. Paul, and the hollow sound of a boat whistle echoes between the river bluffs.

They're all dead now—my husband, my only boy, my mother. I have but one dream left: to walk through the carved front door and into the secret world of the Scarlett O'Hara house.

The day of the neighborhood picnic is bright and sunny. With its fountain that bubbles water from two pairs of gargoyles and its lush green lawns bordered with sculptured hedges, Victoria Park is a perfect place for a picnic.

When the group coalesces into a half circle of chairs, I notice a broad-shouldered man dressed in solid black, unrelieved except for an amplitude of wavy white hair flowing down to his shoulders beneath a black fisherman's hat. A poet, I think. Or a cleric. He looks about my age—late sixties, maybe older. Jenny, one of my neighbors, follows my gaze.

"That's Colin Malloy. He lives in the big house with the white pillars. Kind of a hermit. Wife walked out on him a few years back, and he never got over it. He was a lawyer before he retired, just like his dad."

The gray ghosts of my youthful dreams emerge, jolted out of long years forgetfulness. "I'd love to see his house. Inside, I mean." I envision marble fireplaces, parquet floors, crystal chandeliers and Louis Quatorze furniture with brocade covers.

Jenny frowns and brushes a wisp of gray hair off her cheek. "Colin Malloy's a very private person. Why don't you go on one of Bill Brandt's house tours? That way, you'll see most of the houses around the park." How could I explain a childhood dream? Jenny is one of those practical people who is unforgiving of dreamers.

I imagine Colin Malloy living the life of the idle rich— cruising in the Caribbean, mountain climbing in the Himalayas or drinking cocktails at an expensive hotel like the Cabana del Sol in Puerto Vallarta, where John and I went on our honeymoon.

The memory of John makes me sad again. Pieces of the past cling to me like barnacles on a sinking ship—memories and regrets, weighing me down. I ask Jenny if she knows anyone who has seen Colin's house.

"No, Gina, I haven't. And I don't know anyone who has. I've heard a few stories from people who knew people who've seen it. They say the house looks just as it did in 1900, when Colin's grandparents had it decorated by an interior decorator they flew in from Paris."

Colin Malloy looks bored. He could get up and walk away at any moment, and I wouldn't see him again until next summer, or maybe not then. This could be my last chance to see his house, if there's a chance at all. I'm not comfortable with strangers, so I rehearse what I'm going to say.

He leans back in his chair and watches me walk toward him. His eyes are a vivid blue, his features symmetrical and ageless as a Grecian marble, his expression, remote. I introduce myself; then, suddenly, words escape me, and for an agonizing few moments, I am mute as a stringless harp. What am I doing here, asking a perfect stranger to invite me into his home?

"And you're the lucky person who lives in that beautiful white house?" It sounds asinine, but it's all I can think of on short notice. I've never been noted for sparkling repartee.

"Guilty as charged. With Lancelot," he says. "My cat."

"I love cats." I'm convinced that a man who likes cats has much to recommend him and might even understand why I'd want to see his house.

In a breathless cascade of words, I pour out my fantasies. I tell him how we walked the three miles to the park on warm summer days and sat on the stone bench and pretended we lived in his house. I describe the desolation of Victoria Park in the 1960's, before urban renewal—the weeds in the front yards, the empty lots with their broken foundations, the houses with peeling paint—does he remember? He nods absently, and I wonder if he's still sitting there because he can't easily escape. In spite of that, I blunder on.

"I'd love to see your house," I say. "I know that people who own historic houses enjoy showing them off, because they're such a source of pride and satisfaction." The last words are a last-minute inspiration. I brace myself for his refusal.

"I'm sure we can arrange it," he says. "Let me know when you'd like to come." He takes a notebook out of his pocket and writes something on a slip of paper, rips it out and hands it to me. "My e-mail address," he says.

"Send me a message when you've chosen a convenient time."

Weeks pass. Winter comes and wraps my world in a white blanket of snow. I can see Colin's house if I stand in exactly the right place and look out my front window. Old ghosts rise up to haunt me—the ghosts of my last failed relationships, of my husband, John, of my mother, who would not have approved of my asking for access to a stranger's house. I have nothing in common with Colin Molloy except humanity, and I'm not sure that his humanity is at all like mine.

Summer turns into fall, and the trees in the park change to red and yellow, and some stay stubbornly green. I've begun to miss my garden, my neighbors, my other life. Last year I was cutting down plants after the first frost, taking out stakes, mounding dirt.

The park people come with their big machines, sweep the sidewalks, and drain the fountain, so nothing is left in the concrete basin except a few dead leaves, which, like my memories, are all swept away.

I begin to feel lonely. Being lonely has nothing to do with being alone; it has to do with not having anyone who understands what you have to say. My condo building is populated with young teachers, a journalist, a newspaper editor, and a college administrator, not to mention the young couple upstairs who alternate overnights at "her place" and "his place." She once told me that they have just celebrated two years of "being together." How could she understand my suddenly losing John? He and I had spent thirty years being together, sharing a home, having two children, losing one, all with no alternating overnights to relieve stressful times.

Mother understood once, when we were still speaking. Then, a time came when she stopped understanding and later, stopped speaking, and she couldn't remember who I was. I fixed her meals and combed her hair, and bought groceries and cleaned her house. John was dead by then, and suddenly, there was no one left to understand except a shadow of the person my mother once was.

In November, I gather up my courage and send Colin Malloy an e-mail reminding him of his invitation. When a week passes without an answer, I think he must have changed his mind. But three days later, he responds:

> Gina, I've just returned from a trip to France. When I received your e-mail, I remembered the lady with the lovely smile, and I was sorry it took me so long to respond. Friday evening would be fine for a visit, if it's okay for you.
>
> Colin

I stare at the signature. "Colin." When I answer, I put "Colin" as my salutation, though it seems inappropriate. A person who lives in that kind of house should be called Rhett or Ashley.

When I see Colin's front light go on at seven o'clock on Friday, I walk across the park, past the black outline of the fountain with its snow-capped gargoyles, and up Colin's front steps. The view from the portico is breathtaking: to the east, the river winds around downtown St. Paul. To the west, the lights of the High Bridge stretch across the river like beads on a rosary.

Colin is wearing jeans and a plaid shirt when he answers the door. A large black cat with green eyes stands beside him and looks at me with that judgmental look all cats have. When I reach down to pet him, he puts his ears back and retreats. Colin smiles.

"He doesn't take to strangers," Colin says. "He's had a hard life as a stray."

"He doesn't like me. I love cats. John—my husband—didn't like them, and he wouldn't let me have one."

"A pity. Well, let's proceed."

The entry opens on two rooms: to the left, a living room, and to the right, a study. Neither is what I expect, not the museum-like perfection of antique furnishings—no loveseats or sofas with tapestry covers or antimacassars on Queen Anne chairs with high backs. Except for the anachronism of a TV set in the living room, the house reflects the aesthetics of its owners—a modern sofa, a leather recliner, an oriental rug, and fringed

Victorian lamps with silk shades and wrought-iron bases.

Two brass cherubs holding torches stand guard on each side of an ornate gray marble fireplace. Victorian wallpaper with faded flowers and gilt stripes adorns the walls and plays host to an assortment of ancestors in gilded frames. At the far end of the room, a grandfather clock of ancient vintage laboriously chimes seven.

As we walk from room to room, Colin evokes images of the house's past—the coming of the railroad with trains belching black smoke, the copper roof that his great-grandfather installed to protect the house from the sparks spewed out by passing trains which ignited the dry grass and raced up the hill, the immigrant community along the river banks, the grocery store with freshly-made pasta and hard-crusted bread.

"And the floods. You wouldn't believe the floods that came some years. The waves tore through the homes on the Levee down there and turned yards into ponds. Upper Landing, the city fathers call it."

We walk through a room with a gray marble fireplace flanked by rows of leather-bound books with titles stamped in gold on their spines: *The Iliad, The Odyssey, The Conquest of Peru.* An oil painting of a lady with a white bonnet and soulful eyes gazes down at us.

"My grandmother," Colin says. He turns on a lamp shaped like three calla lilies and tells me his grandmother was fond of "anything Tiffany."

Lancelot and I follow Colin into the dining room. "The stained glass window above the buffet—that's by Tiffany, also. It's beautiful when the sun shines through it."

We make a small procession upstairs—first Colin, then Lancelot, then me. Colin stops and opens a door. The master bedroom has a tan marble fireplace, a massive oak bed and a matching dresser and chiffonier with ornate carvings. Everything is in perfect order. "This was my parents' bedroom," he says.

When we reach the end of the hall, he opens the last door. "My favorite room. It was—well, what people call a party room now, I guess. My parents had their parties here. My brother and I played here when we were kids—when my parents weren't home, of course."

He touches a light switch, and I catch my breath. A mural stretches across one wall from the ceiling down to the wainscoting. I see armored knights on horseback and ladies in ermine-tipped gowns,

"Like it?"

"It's gorgeous. Who painted it?"

"Probably some local artist trying to justify his existence in a world that didn't appreciate him. My mother hated the sight of it—" Colin's voice fades, and he looks away.

"The faces look like real people."

"The Sergeant-at-law and the Prioress—they're my parents. See—the artist put a banner beneath each figure. Dad was a lawyer. Brilliant man."

The Sergeant and the Prioress are richly dressed: the Sergeant in a blue velvet cloak trimmed with ermine, the nun in a wine-colored cape. She wears a turquoise necklace and a matching bracelet.

"But how could you have a prioress for a mother? She's a nun, isn't she?"

Colin chuckled. "I guess the artist thought the Prioress' personality was like my mother's." He points to the inscription beneath the Prioress:

> She was at pains to counterfeit the look
> Of courtliness, and stately manners, too.

"The artist made your family into characters from *The Canterbury Tales*. How clever! This mural—it's meant to be a family portrait, then." It didn't put Colin's mother in a very good light, I thought. "And there—the lady with the big hat—the Wife of Bath?"

> She'd been respectable throughout her life,
> With five churched husbands bringing joy and strife,
> Not counting other company in youth;
> But thereof there's no need to speak, in truth.

"Now, who would that be?" Then I remembered Jenny's comment and wished I hadn't asked. His wife, of course—the wife who left him. Colin shrugs and looks away.

"And the knight in armor? The one in the center who's looking right at us?"

"My brother Aidan."

I move in closer so I can read the banner beneath the knight's horse. "But where are *you*?"

"Here." He points to a crowd of pilgrims. A slim young man in an embroidered tunic and a pale green cape looks up at the Prioress. "Me, when I was sixteen," Colin says.

The squire holds some flowers in his outstretched hand, but the Prioress stares straight ahead, indifferent to the boy's offering. "Life changes one, doesn't it. I was idealistic in those days. Idealistic and hopeful. Not many dreams left now."

I ask Colin if I can take some pictures and show them to some of the local artists. Maybe one might recognize the anonymous artist's work.

"I've never researched it. Tracking the artist down would be an interesting project," Colin says. "Sure—come back tomorrow morning and take all the pictures you want. Coffeepot will be on. Hope you like blueberry scones. And we can talk."

The next morning, I go back and have coffee and blueberry scones with Colin. He listens when I talk to him, and asks questions, as if he wants to understand what I have to say. Time passes too swiftly. He tells me to come back soon, because he wants to hear the results of my research.

"In a couple of days, maybe?' he says.

Jim Arnold at the Historical Society is an expert on nineteenth and twentieth century area artists, but he can't identify the artist or even make an intelligent guess as to the artist's identity. I'm disappointed, but hopeful. My search has just begun.

Weeks pass. I'm referred to people all over St. Paul and Minneapolis— local artists, restoration specialists, even antique dealers. I visit Colin twice a week at first, then three times. He listens intently when I tell him whom I spoke to and what I had learned. We drink tea and eat scones. Colin likes scones. And I'm beginning to like Colin.

One day in April, I tell him how much I miss my garden. He says his mother had a garden "out back," and I'd be welcome to plant some flowers there.

Six months pass—six months of reading art books, talking to people, drinking tea and eating scones with Colin. I learn nothing about the painting, but my visits with Colin are the highlight of my week, so I postpone telling him that I've failed in my search for the artist.

When I tell Jenny about my problem, she says that I've been looking for the mysterious painter in the wrong places, because most artists in the area *"don't know diddly-squat about historical houses or what's in them. Bunch of losers,"* she says. *"Ask Bill Brandt, the local house historian, what he knows about the painting."* She doesn't say "if" he knows; she says "what."

I'd forgotten about Bill Brandt. All summer he led groups of people on tours of the Victoria Park houses. When I call to ask him about Colin's mural, he laughs.

"Oh, yeah. I don't need to look at it. Or at your pictures. I've seen Colin's painting a couple of times. He wanted to know if I thought it was any good. Can you believe it? Colin's a talented guy."

"Colin? You're talking about Colin Malloy?"

"He wanted to be an artist, but his mother wouldn't hear of it. She was paying the bills, so she made the rules: Colin had to study law and join the family law firm, just as Aidan had done. That didn't stop Colin from painting in his spare time, though. He took art classes and painted up a storm. Exhibited his paintings at art shows and sold them in galleries. Got quite a few commissions, too. He's very talented. I'm surprised that you saw the mural, though."

"Why?"

"Last I heard, his mother had hired a couple of paperhangers to cover it up."

The realization of what Colin had done hit me hard. All those weeks pouring through books and records and talking to people, and all the while, I'm on a wild goose chase, courtesy of Colin Malloy.

"Didn't Colin tell you that he painted that mural? Strange. He's a straightforward kind of guy. A bit eccentric, maybe. More so since he lost his wife."

"I'll never forgive Colin for this. Never."

"Hey, don't take it too hard. Colin's a modest guy. He keeps a very low profile. Maybe it was just a practical joke—no? Well, maybe he just liked having you around. I'm sure he gets lonesome in that big house. It's ten years since his wife left him. He took it hard. Swore he'd never get involved with anyone again."

The next day Colin sends me two e-mails, one asking if I still want to plant flowers in the garden, and if I do, we'd better get going on it; the other, asking how my research is coming. I'm torn between not answering at all or sending him a scathing response. Finally, after a month of silence, I send him an e-mail:

> Colin,
>   How could you let me spend six months on a wild goose chase? I suppose you thought that was a good joke. I think it was deceptive and mean-spirited.
>   Gina

A few days pass before he answers:

>   I tilled the back garden rectangle and added some black dirt and compost, and I told the workmen to be careful not to destroy the peonies. You said you loved peonies, didn't you?
>   If you don't want to plant anything, it's okay. I can always have them lay sod over it. Shall I do that?
>   Colin

I walk to the overlook a few days later and watch the *Harriet Bishop* on its way up to Fort Snelling. Out of the corner of my eye, I see Colin sitting on a bench in his back yard. Behind him, a sprinkler throws a fan-shaped stream of water across the lawn.

"Hello!" he yells.

I'm not in favor of people yelling at each other across wide spaces, so I walk over to the bench.

"You thought that was quite a joke, didn't you—making me run all over town to find an anonymous artist. Some anonymous. Why?"

"Maybe I just enjoyed having you around. Then, again, why did it take you so long to tell me you couldn't find anything? You didn't seem to mind eating my scones. In fact, you looked as if you liked being here as much as I enjoyed having you. So, what about the garden? You want to plant some flowers, or not? It would be a shame to let all of that nice black dirt go to waste."

I see that the garden plot has been freshly tilled. What could be better than a garden that overlooks a river. I can feel the dirt between my fingers and see the flowers—lilies and scabiosa and hollyhocks, and—

"Roses grow well there," Colin says. "Lots of sun. Those peony bushes along the side will bloom again, too, with some care. They're red, I think. Well, no, not all. Some pink ones, too. And some white. Peony bushes are some of the few things in life you can count on."

He stares out the window, remembering. "We could plant some rose bushes out there. And daisies. I like daisies."

"We?"

"Oh, I suppose I could help, but I don't like dirt under my fingernails." He holds his hands out in front of him. His fingers are long and tapered. The hands of an artist. I lean down to pet Lancelot, who is rubbing his chin against my leg.

"See, he likes you. It just takes him awhile to decide if he can trust you. Lance and I—we don't take to people right off."

"Why did you let me waste all of that time? Why didn't you tell me that it was your painting?"

"I got the feeling, from a few things you said when we drank all of that coffee—I got the feeling that you were feeling sorry for yourself. It worked, didn't it? Gave you something to do? Besides, it was kind of nice having you around. I'm sure you wouldn't have spent all of that time with me otherwise—would you?" He leans back in his chair and looks away. The daylight is fading. A barge carrying a load of lumber makes its way downriver.

"You painted your brother as a knight in shining armor. Was he—like that?"

Colin looks away. I follow his gaze. Across the yard, a cardinal emerges from a lilac bush and flies up ino a tree. "My mother thought so. I took care of her—at the end. I was with her when she—when my mother died, but she never said my name. She called out *his* name—Aiden—Aiden, and cried when he didn't come. Aiden was dead—died the year before. I tried to tell her, at first, but she didn't understand. Or want to understand. So I stopped trying. He was the one she wanted beside her, not me. That's the way it always was, even when we were kids." He turns away. We sit without speaking. An eagle dips and rises again above the bluffs to the south, then disappears. Colin stands up suddenly and walks toward the house. "Guess I'll put the coffeepot on."

I watch the sprinkler oscillate back and forth in a wide arc, the leaves on the lilac bush trembling at each round. A goldfinch flies across the yard, circles, then perches on a thistle seed feeder a few yards away.

"Well, then, let's drink to our garden."

"It has to be sweet."

He holds the door open, closes it behind me and walks to the fridge. "Sweet. H'm-m. There's orange juice here. How about we have fuzzy navels? No, we don't have peach schnapps. A fuzzy navel is nothing without the schnapps." He pulls a tray of ice cubes out of the fridge and takes two glasses down from the cupboard. "I guess it's scotch and soda. Okay?"

We sit at the kitchen table. A large window gives us a view of the back yard and the plowed-up space where the garden is going to be. I see roses and hollyhocks and daisies in full bloom, and two rows of foxglove swaying in the breeze. Colin reaches across the table and takes my hand.

"Memories?"

"No, not memories. Visions."

"Visions are better," he says. "They signal hope instead of regret."

JILL C. ALT

YES,

I will turn to mist and blow away forever, and
Yes, I will come back if you beckon and hold you
Till the normal rings and everyday begins.

Yes, I will love your children as if born to me, and
Yes, I will make a distance, a space of memory
Where their mother may speak to each alone.

Yes, I will listen to you, further, I will hear you, and
Never will a day go by when I am nowhere near you
Even over miles and storms and doubts and dereliction.

Yes, there are no other gods, no other men, no other tunes, and
Yes, the time is endless unless it isn't, unless it's soon.
And yes, whatever it is you ask, the answer will be yes.

ANNA CHANCE

IN MY 70TH YEAR

I am starting over. Questions arise, with whom? My friend saw my aloneness. She suggested a possibility…she knew another single.

He answered the challenge and phoned me with casual conversation. We decided to meet in the coming week for coffee and cake.

It is snowing and I hesitate beside each store window, unable to see who I am in the dim reflection, sensing changes in my life. I don't want to be late. I make my decision and enter the restaurant in a flurry of snow and bravado. Eleanor Roosevelt said, "One ought to do something scary every day." I just did and he is not here yet. That is scary. A man alone is coming in the door. We smile. He's the one. We drink coffee for two hours.

He asks, "So, would you like to do something together?"

The wary ritual has begun. I say, "Yes, yes I would…I like your face."

He, "Well, I like your face also. I'll call."

Our rendezvous is a theater parking lot. He is late. That is scary. May be I'm early. After the movie, drinks and talk, he says he'll call.

After another movie, more talk and drinks, he suggests a jazz club for our next date. Good choice. Nice evening, I feel quite fetching in my modern low cut blouse. Suddenly, in the car, a moment of truth, he reaches for a breast to kiss. My flirty mood is challenged by reality. Fight or flight? Cool prevails.

I calmly say, "Don't you think this is rather forward?"

He mumbles with lips full, "No, I watched you all evening. This needs doing." I realize old guys don't fool around. A simple goodnight kiss follows. "I'll call," he says.

Our next date is a concert. Afterwards, not caring for the bar scene, I say, "Come see my house, I've no furniture, the remodeling is done…I've got some scotch." Clever me, I have his favorite brand. No chairs, no couch, no bed, no TV, so we sit on my new fur rug. Be still my heart, remember I'm

70. We're both 70, but the night is young. We relapse into an easy make-love mood. Two years a widow, have I forgotten how? "Yes, I'd like to try."

He is divorced many years, without a lover for some time.

Big question I ask, "Condoms, anyone?"

"No," he says, "I'm healthy. I give blood every two months."

Ach! Oh well, take a chance; we are 70, made it this far. "I'm leaving my socks on. I have (ha, ha) cold feet."

He says, "Good, same for me, But I want to see you naked."

I acquiesce. After all, that is what fur rugs are for. Oh, my lord, it is marvelous to be held again and kissed and fondled, etc.

Later, he says, "I'll call."

I wonder, he had his way, he saw me naked, vulnerable. Will he call or is it over now? I wait. I ruminate. He probably will call, after all we laughed about the rug, the hard floor and our arthritis. He said I should consider a bed, 'easier on knees'.

I hurry to put up my bed and drapes. Move in the new furniture, hang pictures, clean the bathroom, sing out loud, "I'm so, so cool."

I'm coy with my friends. "Yes, we've been to a few movies." I think about our conversations. He is the serious type, very intelligent. I try to be. He is very muscular, a cyclist. I realize I must resume exercising. We never discuss money, politics yes, money no. He works weekends. I'm retired except for being a writer and poet. Now, I have a gentleman caller....

I'm surprised at the intensity of our lovemaking, like time gone backward. We go to my house; his bathroom is being remodeled. Our dates seem to happen suddenly, usually weeknights. Nothing was planned for Valentine's Day. He calls at the last minute. Says, "Church got out early, let's hit the jazz club." I buy a valentine, just in case. He didn't. I put my gift back for some other time. He seems proud and independent. I don't want to pressure him; I never phone him.

He says, "I like modern, independent women." Another time, discussing clothing, I mention the desire to wear glamorous clothes. He says he prefers elegant. I do not believe this matters at the movies or clubs we attend. Still, I bought a few more elegant outfits. I smile. I am a chameleon and like the Ray Price song,

> I'll never know till it's over,
> If it's right or it's wrong loving you.

But I'd rather be sorry for something I've done,
Than for something that I didn't do

Our lovemaking is getting longer and better. He tells me it will be better when I learn to relax. I tell him that he is a "beautiful man". There! I bet no one ever told him that before. He says we'll go dancing after his lessons are finished. I remind him I have an RV and large acreage on the lake. He says we'll go sailing; there's a sailboat in his driveway. He's beginning to call for no reason. We talk about our sore necks. He wants to know what I'm doing. I mention mundane chores and finishing my taxes. Why am I not more vague or inventive?

One evening after lovemaking that was all I'd dreamed of and some not dreamed, I told him I thought his general attitude a bit too distant, or aloof, no, I mean guarded.

He nodded yes and said, "I'm always guarded. I won't be hurt again. I'll never fall in love again."

I smiled. "That's understandable. I'll never re-marry. If you stick around awhile you'll learn what a good friend I am."

He said, "I'll call."

Recently, as he prepared to leave, I asked, (jokingly) "Will I see you again?"

He paused at the door, "Well, yes…again and again. You'll probably become tired of me." He grinned and disappeared into the dark of my porch.

Leaning back on my couch, I felt that might be some sort of commitment.

On reflection, I shall always be in a state of love. Other men in my life I've loved in different ways. Now, he-who-is-guarded won't know if I love him or not. I'm full of love. I love my dog, my house, my grandchildren, their parents, and the sun on my patio, the rain, the bright cold New Year that brought me this new affair. I'll pass this way but once and intend to love the life I am making. I shall not deny love; it comes in many forms and circumstances. Sometimes taking a chance is all right. This lesson is well learned at age seventy. I remain cautiously optimistic.

WAYNE SCHEER

THE FLOWERS ON BLOOM STREET

Jack Ruszkowski sat by himself in a nearly empty restaurant blowing on his lukewarm coffee. He took a noisy sip and replaced the cup to its saucer. Staring at the age spots on the back of his unsteady hands, he looked up at the empty seat across from him and mumbled, "Remember when freckles used to be cute?"

A heavyset, middle-aged woman and her husband seated at a table nearby turned his way. The woman smiled at Jack in the closed lip manner usually reserved for children.

"Sorry," he said, with a wave of his hand. He returned to his already cold omelet. Yellow had oozed from it when he took his first bite, and the melted cheese and egg now congealed on his plate. Edith's omelets never ran, he thought. Picking at it in a futile attempt to avoid the onions, he tried recalling if he had told the waitress no onions.

He and Edith rarely went out for breakfast. Fifty-two years, he thought, if we were home, Edith made breakfast. "What?" he could hear her ask. "We need to pay someone to scramble an egg for us? If I go out, I want something I don't make at home."

Now Jack ate most of his meals out.

After sipping a little more coffee, he stood up, uttering an involuntary "ugghh" as his joints snapped loud enough to again attract the attention of the middle-aged couple. He began his trek to the cash register, dragging his feet. His ankles stiffened whenever he sat for a period of time. Already, he thought, I do the old man shuffle, with my own musical accompaniment. He considered offering his little joke to the couple staring at him, but feared they'd only offer another patronizing smile.

The waitress who had served him now stood behind the register. He handed her the check and the exact sum of money with which to pay it. She asked if he enjoyed his meal. Although he knew she didn't care, he told her anyway. "The omelet was a little runny. They should cook the eggs more."

He saw her smile and sensed she was going to wish him a good day, without hearing what he had said. Then a look of recognition came over her face. "Next time, honey, say you want your omelet well done."

The condescension in her voice annoyed him. "Who likes runny eggs in an omelet? I never knew I had to say, 'please cook the eggs.'"

"Have a nice day," the waitress said.

He turned and pushed open the restaurant door, smelling the fresh morning air. Yes, it's a nice day. I should walk. He knew his ankles would feel better after a walk. His back, too. Besides, there was no reason to rush home. Instead of turning right and walking less than one block to his apartment, Jack turned left, passing Wakeman and Son Florist. He used to buy Edith a dozen red roses for her birthday, every October 14. On her fiftieth birthday, he had Mr. Wakeman make a special arrangement for her. It cost him twice as much as the roses.

"They were out of roses?" Edith asked. "This is nice, too."

He never bought her anything but a dozen roses after that.

His ankles felt much better. He could bend his foot now. All things considered, he was in pretty good shape for a man of seventy-six, he thought. Edith would have turned seventy-five last October. They planned a cruise to the Bahamas to celebrate. That was before the doctor told them the cancer had spread.

He remembered talking of their plans for her seventy-fifth as he and their son, Darren, sat with her in the hospital.

"One day you plan a trip. The next day…" He never finished the sentence. Instead, he broke down. He had never cried in front of his son before.

That was nearly a year ago. He cried plenty since.

He continued walking down Brandt Street until he came to the corner of Brandt and Stanton, and turned right on Stanton. This was always a nice street, he thought. Old trees, probably oaks. Soon after he retired he had bought an identifying guide to plants, trees and flowers. He and Edith took a walk through Brunswick Park with their book. "This is a sycamore tree," he remembered Edith shouting, looking momentarily like the young woman he married. "See how big the leaves are."

Jack wondered what had happened to the book.

A wave of sadness came over him. He felt it in the back of his throat, and held back tears. "Of all the things in my life to regret? Not learning the difference between an oak and a sycamore." He looked around to make sure no one overheard him talking to himself.

Now he turned the corner to see the flowers people had planted in the little strips of land separating the well-kept two story brownstones from the sidewalk. He looked up and realized he was on Bloom Street. "A good name," he said aloud, smiling.

"Good day to you," a young man wearing a gray suit and carrying a briefcase said as he hurried by.

Jack wanted to stop the man and show him the flowers that people had planted and how the name of the street was Bloom Street, but he knew the man would just smile politely and say something like, "Well isn't that interesting," not wanting to talk with a crazy old man.

He missed being able to go home and tell Edith what he had observed. She probably wouldn't care either, he knew that, but at least she'd listen. Then she'd tell him what her sister had said about her daughter-in-law, and he wouldn't care, but he'd listen. That was what he missed most about marriage. It wasn't what he and Edith talked about; it was caring about the other person enough to listen.

Everyone's in a rush, he thought. Off to do the next thing. It's not until you don't have a next thing to do that you see the flowers on Bloom Street. Jack laughed. I've become a philosopher in my old age.

Jack recalled having this same thought the first Sunday after he retired. He had begun thinking about the long workweek ahead of him, and getting that queasy feeling in the pit of his stomach. Then he remembered he had nothing planned for Monday and he took a long, deep sigh of relief. That was how he should feel now, he thought. After spending almost six months caring for Edith as she wasted away, he now had nothing to do. Until this moment, he had felt empty and lost. For the first time since her death, he admitted to himself that he also felt relieved.

"I have nothing I have to do today," he said aloud. Two young girls jumping rope looked at him with their heads tilted sideways. One pointed her index finger to her head and made circles in the air. They both laughed.

He laughed with them, and for a moment considered asking if he could skip rope, too. But he didn't want to intrude on their fun. Besides, he knew he'd probably break his neck if he tried.

Jack guessed he had been walking for almost an hour. He was tired, but he still felt no urge to go home. Instead, he decided to cut down Elton Boulevard, a neighborhood of older brick apartment buildings. He hadn't been down that street in years.

He remembered a recurring nightmare he had as a kid. He'd be walking home from school or church, something he'd done a million times, and suddenly the streets all seemed different and he'd be lost. He wasn't afraid of that happening now. Not yet, at least. He had lived in this neighborhood for over thirty years. He knew it like the back of his own hand.

Of course, he still saw the back of his hand as smooth and firm. With freckles, not age spots.

Ahead of him, carrying a bag of groceries, was Mrs. Hegel. Sam Hegel and, what was her name? Karla? They went to the same church as he and Edith. That was a long while ago. Sam was dead for what? It must be four years now, at least.

"I see you talking to yourself," she said, laughing. "Your lips are moving."

He smiled, a little embarrassed. He would have tipped his hat if he wore one because he felt so good seeing a familiar face. "It's been a long time, Karla. How are you?"

She smiled back. "So long, you forgot my name. It's Katherine. My friends call me Katie now."

They laughed and tried to remember the last time they saw one another. "It was in church. Before Sammy got sick," she said. "I remember how you and Sammy would sleep every Sunday morning. Edith and I would just shake our heads." She smiled. "How is Edith? I haven't seen her in some time."

Jack lowered his eyes. "Edith passed almost a year ago."

"Oh, I'm so sorry." She reached out and touched his arm reassuringly. Jack felt a shiver. He had forgotten how long it had been since he felt the hand of a woman who wasn't taking his blood pressure. "I stopped going to St. Peter's," she continued. "Too many memories there. I thought it would do me some good to start over. Besides, even old friends aren't comfortable with a single woman. Afraid I might steal their husbands." She smiled, showing a set of unnaturally white teeth.

He watched her shift the bag of groceries from one arm to the other. "Here. Let me take that bag," he said, reaching for it.

"I live just two doors down," she said, clutching the bag to her chest.

"Then even at my age I can manage." He took the bag from her. "Managing is what I do now." He meant it as a joke, but he feared it sounded more like a whine.

When they got to her apartment, she suggested he come in for a cup of coffee.

"That would be good, but I just had some at the diner on Brandt Street." He wondered how honest he could be with her. He decided to go for it. "What I really need is to use your bathroom. It was almost an hour ago when I had coffee."

"An hour? You must be busting. Come in."

She fumbled with her purse until she found the key.

The apartment was overheated, but inviting. The walls were painted a light rose color. It felt like a home, neat and clean, but a faint odor of yesterday's pot roast lingered. That's what he missed in his own home, he realized. It had been a long while since he smelled yesterday's dinner.

"Put the bag down on the counter," she said, pointing to the kitchen. "And go use the bathroom."

He did as she said, observing how spotless the kitchen was except for one coffee cup in the sink.

She showed him the way to the toilet. "Please forgive the mess. I wasn't expecting company." She spoke in a voice that appeared to Jack to be begging for a compliment.

He offered one. "Mess? You could eat off the floors. Your home is beautiful, Katherine."

"Katie."

In the bathroom, Jack was careful to lift the toilet seat and aim at the side of the bowl, not directly into the water, to avoid making too much noise. Afterwards, he washed his hands, unsure if he should dry them on the towels folded neatly beside the sink. Knowing he could never refold them properly, he chose to shake off the excess water and wipe his hands on the side of his pants. Taking a comb from his pocket, he combed his hair from one side to the other in an effort to cover his bald spot.

"I put up a fresh pot of coffee," Katie said. "At least it'll taste like coffee, not like what they serve at the diner." She had already laid out a plate of butter cookies, the ones with a little cherry in the middle that Edith used to buy at Barrone's Bakery.

Jack had never thought of Katherine Hegel, Katie, as an attractive woman, but he never really looked at her before. Now he saw a woman who kept herself looking as good as she could. Heavy, but not fat, she was the kind of woman Jack's generation called "ample." Jack now found her attractive.

As they spoke about their new lives since the death of their mates, Jack heard in her voice sadness, but not self-pity. She had gone through dark times, she told him, but now she preferred light. As if to underscore her point, Jack noticed she had opened the blinds when he was in the bathroom. The morning sun peeked in through the slats, tentatively at first, but now light filled the apartment.

He also noticed something about Katie he had never seen before. A small butterfly tattoo on her upper arm. He couldn't help but stare at it.

"This was my present to myself on the one year anniversary of Sammy's death. It reminds people there's more to me than just being a widow." She paused and winked at Jack. "If Sammy ever knew I got it, he'd die all over again."

Jack wasn't sure how to react, but when he saw Katie's open-mouthed laugh, he relaxed and laughed with her.

He even shared with her his observation that there were more flowers on Bloom Street than anywhere else in the neighborhood. She appeared impressed, saying she'd have to look the next time she went that way.

"If you like flowers," she said, "we should go to the Botanical Gardens. Thursday, after four, admission is free for seniors."

When it was time to go, Jack asked her if she'd like to join him for supper at China Inn. Instead, she suggested he come back tonight for a pot roast she had in the refrigerator. "I have so much left over, it would be a shame to waste it."

On his way home, Jack saw two boys, about ten, playing catch with a tennis ball. "Over here," he yelled to the boys. "Let's see how good your arm is."

The boy holding the ball threw it over Jack's head. He ran back a few steps and jumped as high as he could, his arms extended to the sky. To his amazement, he felt the ball land squarely in the palm of his hand.

"Nice catch, Mister," the boys shouted as he threw the ball back to them. He put just enough behind his throw to remind himself that he still had some life left in the old arm.

CYNTHIA SAMPLE

THE PRAYERS OF DOREEN NEWTON

Monday

Dear God,

Pastor says we should build up our faith by writing out our prayers and their answers. I doubt it'll do much good. Mostly since Harry died, all the answers seem to be NO! But that's what Pastor says, so here goes, God.

First of all, the garage door has warped some more. You of all people —well You're not a *people* I don't guess, but anyway—You ought to know that I can't afford a contractor. So I'm asking You right now: how do I fix my garage door for $100?

Hmmm...hmmm...hmmm....

So now I think You want me to call Richard. Harry hired him to build the storage room and Richard needed the money. Maybe he can fix it.

Tuesday

Dear God,

I wish Richard would stop all that noise—every time another one of those boards falls down, I near 'bout jump out of my stockings. But God, You're getting my garage fixed. Now, if You could make everyone stay home while I drive to the bank for the money to pay Richard, I'd really appreciate it. I can't lose my license what with Harry gone and all.

Later

Dear God,

Help! Richard just said he's been thinking about me ever since his Esther died. He's asking to come over here for a decent meal—said he hasn't had one since Esther and her kitchen went their separate ways. He does look pretty thin. On TV yesterday, there was that story about Mother Teresa—are

You sending me a sign?

Now I'm having an idea & I'll bet it's from You. I'll cook him up something and just send it on home with him. Things have changed—men expect things of you when you have a date nowadays. I'll fix up some chicken and dumplings; that'll keep til he gets home.

Wednesday

Dear God,

What'll I do now? Richard called up to thank me for the chicken and dumplings. Now he says he loves me. "Well, you're welcome," I said. But then he said it again, only louder. He wants to come on over here tonight. I didn't know *what* to say, so I answered: "Well, all right."

God, help me out of this!! I couldn't say: "Richard, I don't love *you*," so soon after Esther just died. That could hurt his feelings. I wouldn't know what to say to a man that wasn't Harry. Alone, I mean. You stopped the traffic when I went to the bank yesterday. Now You gotta fix this! I pray that he NOT—I repeat NOT—come over here.

Later

God,

Richard called to say his car won't start. "Guess our little date will just have to wait, honey." He actually called me 'honey,' which Harry never did. Anyway, thank you that Richard isn't coming over here—and I do hope he gets his car fixed eventually.

Speaking of Harry, God—I hope You bless him wherever he is in heaven. Be sure to give him something to do—You know he always got bored; we always had that in common. And don't let him know about Richard. I'd hate to spoil things for Harry even the slightest little bit. You know Harry always was the jealous type. Why, I remember...well, God, You probably remember too, although I'll bet it doesn't make You blush.

So here's my prayer: keep this pie from tipping over on the floorboard while I get it over to Richard's. I'll put it on his porch and just ring the bell. Even my mama didn't insist on a chaperone in broad daylight on the street. I don't want Richard to feel bad, God. I just don't want him calling me honey and coming over here.

<u>Thursday</u>

Dear God,

Who'd have thought, with that run-down shack, that Richard could get his car fixed in ONE DAY. He said he prayed about it, but I don't believe him. No one could live in that mess and be a praying person. Am I just being judgmental? Maybe his wife did everything and he's just...well, you know, stupid about real life, like most men. Even Harry, bless his heart.

Here's the reason for this prayer, God: Richard called first thing this morning and he wants to come over today. God, you've got to get me out of this. But don't—I repeat, DON'T—let anything happen to his car again. He can't afford it.

<u>Later</u>

Here I am again, God. You HAVE to stop doing things to Richard. I didn't want him to fall off his porch, to get *hurt*. Heal that sprained foot as quick as possible cause he has to work. But DON'T let him come over here. Just don't let anything else bad happen to him.

<u>Friday</u>

God, I haven't heard from Richard, and here it is noon already! Should I call over there? Just tell me what to do and I'll do it. Except I must be honest, at least with You. I don't want him to call me honey—not only because of Harry, but because yesterday, I remembered those dirty old men back in the '50s, always calling us young women 'honey,' and 'sweet-kins.' Burns me up to think about that, even now. Why, like I was a child or a loose woman or something.

<u>Later</u>

Dear God,

Pastor better not expect me to read this prayer journal out loud in Sunday School, because God, you know I CANNOT do that. Especially not after what happened tonight.

I don't know what came over me, God. Pastor says when we put things on paper, we figure them out (sort of like naming our sins). So here goes: when I took that beef stew and that praline cheesecake over to Richard, I <u>only</u> wanted to cheer him up. When I cleaned up his house, it was just because he was hurt and all. And when I overpaid him for fixing my garage door, I was just remembering that it's not easy making your dollars match your hours. I decided it was more important to help out than to have a chaperone. It was like an *executive* decision.

Maybe I should ask you to forgive me, or maybe I shouldn't. I just don't know. All I really wanted was to get my garage door fixed. Now I have to hide things from Pastor cause when Richard lifted his chin and yelled, "Cock-a-doodle-do!" as if he was about to get. . .well, You of all people ought to know. Why, I've plumb had the shivers ever since.

Richard didn't call me honey after I asked him not to. I guess that's an answer to prayer.

ANGELA CONTI MOLGAARD

WHEN ELSIE MARRIED BOB

One day in 1969, my 70-year-old grandmother, Elsie, disappeared from our New Jersey home with two suitcases. Six weeks later, she called us from St, Petersburg, Florida. A few months after that, she had met a man on the street named Bob Rabinof, a recently widowed WWI veteran from Chicago who was 80, partially deaf, and blind. Bob subsequently invited her to his house. They shared a grapefruit from his own tree in the backyard, and he proposed. Elsie wrote, "I know he's older but he's got money and a place to live. I felt sorry for this old man and I like war stories, and besides he's funny."

Soon after marriage there was tension as Elsie wrote us long letters complaining about Bob. He refused to allow her to buy the "expensive" margarine. He sharpened his old razor blades and bought a used hearing aid that didn't work. Elsie said her voice was hoarse from yelling all the time.

But Bob was making an effort to have some fun, enjoy married life and his new companion. He arranged for them to take long bus tours all through the South and Midwest. Elsie sent us postcards from tourist locations and mostly complained, "All we did was stop and support all the Ramada and Holiday Inns." Bob also took her on a cruise to the Caribbean. She wrote, "Why do I need to see all those blacks in Jamaica when I can see them here in my own neighborhood?" Bob even booked a trip to Switzerland but they had to cancel when Bob wasn't feeling well. Elsie was relieved.

We were anxious to meet "Grandpa Bob," who was thrilled to inherit some new grandchildren as he was childless. After they had been married about a year, we drove to Florida to visit the newlyweds in their home, a rambler in a St. Petersburg residential area. Elsie insisted she meet us on a street corner in downtown St. Pete without Bob to alert us to some ground rules. She stood on the appointed corner in a winter coat and scarf, even though it was 85 degrees and sunny. Her first words were, "You never know if there's going to be a breeze." Then she launched into the briefing.

"He's got a quick temper, so don't provoke him. He's a little deaf and doesn't see well. And don't ask about his relatives in Chicago or he'll get angry and don't mention money. He's got $15,000 of WWII bonds stuffed under his mattress for a rainy day; don't turn on the air conditioning as he likes to save money and don't talk on the phone, it's a party line, and besides, the FBI is listening in."

Bob greeted us warmly on the front yard, full head of white hair, thick glasses and cane. We then experienced constant bickering for a week from the newlyweds on every subject from her cooking, her spending, and his irritability. They only stopped when we went on outings. One evening, Bob insisted we join him at the American Legion meeting with other WWI veterans who sang songs like *"Over There"* and tried to dance. Though nearly deaf, Bob could feel the vibration of the music and taught us how to dance the *Lindy* and the *Peabody.*

We went to the beach at Ft. De Soto where Bob wore bathing trunks that were so old that the elastic, obviously worn out, exposed all his equipment as he lay on the beach towel. Meanwhile, Elsie sat in a beach chair wrapped in a coat and a towel around her head, afraid of a breeze. On our way home from the beach, Bob told the bus driver, how much are two kids, me and one "grand maw?" Elsie smirked.

The temperatures and humidity climbed one night and we were stifling in their house without being able to turn on the air conditioning. To make matters worse, Elsie went around in the middle of night throwing wool blankets over us. She saw me wake up sweating and she sat on my bed explaining, without prompting, that she had arranged to have separate rooms when they got married as there wasn't supposed to be any "funny stuff." However, she said, it didn't keep Bob from trying on their wedding night. "He ran after me with his cane through the house naked, with his thing half up." She then continued to tell me about her ex-husband, my grandfather, who she described as "oversexed" and "would come at me with that dry stick." I didn't have much to say as I was only twelve at the time.

Bob used his cane for walking and pointing, among other things. He would use it to lift Elsie's dress up slightly and remark, "She's a woman all right," or tap on the window at noisy neighbors. One time we watched him use it as a hockey stick at the dinner table. He complained Elsie's homemade biscuits were too hard and flicked one in the air slamming it against the wall as it if was a hockey puck.

After dinner and a few beers Bob would launch into a series of incoherent WWI anecdotes from the front where he had befriended "Fritz", a German soldier, who somehow became his drinking buddy. Probably after the Germans surrendered? Bob also told us stories about his hardware store in Chicago and when women would come in and ask for "a screw." This would always bring a frown to Elsie's face.

By the late 1970's, Elsie's letters indicated their marriage was deteriorating rapidly, but she put up with it for a roof over her head, she said. But she had to admit that Bob had a zest for life even at this age and still tried hard to have "relations" with her.

Bob was quite generous with my sister and me, sending us savings bonds for Christmas and birthdays. Elsie was trying to get more money, but she said, "Bob says I shouldn't help anyone over sixteen." He encouraged my sister and me to go to college and get the education he never had. But Elsie was convinced that girls shouldn't go to college and tried to talk us out of it. She would tell us to consider library or school office clerk and once she wrote, "What about Lincoln? No formal education, but the library helped him to be a strong worker. Don't go to Georgetown, it's for lawyers who want to become civil servants who wouldn't be working anyway if it wasn't for Watergate and don't go to college in a big city, all that confusion and ethnic groups, and don't come to Florida, it's too expensive and the liberal boys are dangerous—murders and rapes every day. Love Grandma Elsie"

By 1980, Bob and Elsie were still bickering but something must have changed. She wrote often about his "violent temper" and mentioned once that "Bob is mentally unbalanced and I fear for my life." According to Elsie years later she told us that Bob had or was about to buy a gun and planned a murder/suicide pact which was why suddenly one day, she left the rambler, rented a small apartment downtown, found a local lawyer and filed for divorce.

In February 1981, she was granted the divorce and awarded a $10,000 certificate of deposit and $400 dollars a month alimony which he paid up for only two months.

On June 29, 1981, Bob was sentenced to thirty days in a Pinellas County jail for contempt and refusal to pay the alimony. Within days the story hit not only the local news but major newspapers, including the *Miami Herald, New York Daily News,* and *The New York Times* with headlines like, *"92-Year-old man in jail cell for refusing to pay alimony," "Defiant at 92,"* and

"*He fixed her income. Pays dues instead of alimony.*"

Bob, they wrote, was probably the oldest man in America who had ever been jailed for non-payment of alimony. One reporter actually visited and photographed him in his jail cell where he angrily whacked his cane on the cell's stone floor and was quoted, "I ain't no Dillinger or Capone. This alimony business is a lot of rubbish. I would sit in jail rather than to give it to her." They said the feisty Bob spent his time playing cards and trading candy bars with the other prisoners and paced a mile everyday in his cell. After the thirty days were up he paid the alimony and reluctantly bought his freedom and left the jail in a wheelchair.

He went back to live in his rambler and Elsie met him on the street a few times and even cooked dinner for him once after the divorce. Tragically though, a few years later, some intruders broke into his home looking for money and bludgeoned Bob to death. He was 95.

Elsie returned to New Jersey with her cash settlement and lived to age 96. She summed up the whole experience by saying one day, "I was forced to get married to live a little."

LYNN RUTH MILLER

I HAVE A NEW LOVE EVERY DAY

> Grow old along with me!
> The best is yet to be,
> The last of life for which the first was made.
> Robert Browning

I fall madly in love every day: exciting, buoyant and daring passion that overwhelms me. I love the intensity; I cherish the thrill. I never tire of it. Ever. I am almost seventy-five years old. I have no husband, no partner, no children, and no family. Yet, I am showered with affection, covered with hugs and kisses. I give away my favors freely and often because I know these romances are the kind only an old woman can enjoy.

I am desperately in love with Leo. He visits me every day and gives me sweet kisses. He changes light bulbs and he fixes my front gate. He feeds my puppies and takes me for rides past his old haunts to tell me stories about the days when he was young and I wasn't around. And what do I do to deserve this love?

I exist. Evidently, that is all he wants from me and I am determined to keep existing for a very long time. I don't want to lose all that wonderful attention.

Leo is at least twelve years younger than I and has a lovely wife. Her name is Carol and I love her, too. She sends me little cakes at Easter and platters of food on special holidays. How could I NOT love her?

She gives me knitting advice and shares not just her husband but her son with me. He helps me with my computer and laughs at all my jokes…even when they aren't funny. The fact is that Carol loves me too. She loves that I make her guys feel important when she is too busy at the office or out with her own friends to worry about the state of their emotions.

My dearest sweetie pie is James. He is an engineer at my television station who sees to it that my program set is ready and perfect for filming every single month. James is as loyal to me as any human being can be. When I give a party he is there. When I present a show at our local coffee house, there is James, listening, applauding, encouraging…very, very *there*.

Whenever we have a spare moment in our busy single lives, we go out for a drink…soft drink that is, because James is a recovered alcoholic and does not want to go back where he once was. We talk about nothing much and we hold hands because we love the safety of being with each other. James is 76 years old and has been through several wives. I have discarded a few husbands in my day and we both remember how messy those broken commitments can be. We hug, we kiss, we hold hands and we laugh together, but neither of us would dream of sharing a bed or greeting one another over the breakfast table. We have been there and we have done that with other people in other places. We have had our fill of commitment. We know that the freedom we two have is our lucky charm.

My most adorable and funny love is a guy named Mickey who makes me laugh and treats me to dinners even when he could have a sexy little hottie to take home to bed. He gives up these evenings because he knows how comfortable it is to be with someone who doesn't want him to prove a thing. He is a perfect person to me and I do not want him to change. I want him to be exactly who he is. When Mickey and I go out, he gives away clothing and money to the homeless on street corners. He is not rich, but he always has coins and cash to give to a fellow entertainer in need and he doesn't want thank-yous. He has brought up his son and daughter alone and has done such a marvelous job that they feel proud and happy to be themselves. I think he is a saint. I treasure Mickey for what he teaches *me*, although I am the one who is supposed to be showering wisdom on *him*. I learn from his giving, his compassion and his selflessness; he profits from my persistence, my optimism and my proof that if you live long enough, your happiness can only multiply.

I have a toy boy, too and I am proud of him. His name is Steve and he is not yet thirty. He surfs; he loves women; he once did drugs and struggles not to return to them. He wants to have adventures, become a millionaire, go to the moon. When he goes out with women his age, they make demands he can't fill. They want physical proof that he will adore them forever. They demand, they have tantrums and they weep. They forget to notice how wonderfully perfect he is *because* of his flaws. Steve walks his dog with mine and we discuss stuff. We don't always agree but we laugh a lot and we care. We differ in our politics and in our definition of the good life, but so what? When our walk is over we kiss goodbye and we each go our own way. When we meet again, each of us has grown a little and has added something new to who we are. And that is an exciting thing.

When I was in my teens, I could never get the guy I liked to like me. I was too worried about the pimple on my face, the sag to my bottom and the condition of my page boy bob. When I finally landed a husband, I was consumed with the desire to be the best wife in the universe. I cooked elaborate meals; I cleaned every inch of our apartment. I entertained his friends. I had sex whenever he wanted even if I was in the midst of scrubbing a floor. I even served him breakfast in bed.

And then he left. I was too much for him and I understand that now. During that horrible, tense and mildly hysterical time of my life, I never once asked myself if I *wanted* to cook those dinners, scrub those floors or have sex with this guy who burst into tears when he failed a test and threw things at me when we disagreed. I was too young, too insecure,…too needy.

There were other failed marriages, other shattered romances and I never knew why they didn't work. I wanted love more than anything in the world. I didn't realize that I was putting that well known cart before the horse. First, you meet the person, then you make a friend. Then you fall in love. I cannot repair my unhappy, unfulfilled twenties and thirties… and I wouldn't want to try. I know that I was not in the right place for real romance. I didn't love myself enough to be loved.

Now, I am delighted with me. Lovers flock to my door and I receive them with open arms. Love after seventy is the best kind of bargain because nothing you give feels like it costs. I have never cooked a meal for Leo or James. Mickey and Steve take ME out for dinner. I had Gordon over for a birthday dinner and he walked out without helping me do the dishes! I never invited him back. When my first husband did that, I didn't have the self respect to say, "Hey buster! I cooked…you clean."

When Bob asked me to mend his shirts, I handed them back and told him to buy new ones. I don't need to do that for anyone unless I WANT to.

Lucky me.

I admit it. My lovers come and go like buses on a schedule. I greet them, I adore them and I kiss them good-by at my front door. Then I return to my own quiet bed with my puppies to cuddle and a book to read. Even so, I can barely sleep for excitement. What new Romeo will I discover on my walk through town? What adorable sweetheart will I capture when I open my e-mail?

When you are my age, lovers love loving you because they know you can show them the secret of happiness.

I've told all of my darlings what it is and now I will tell you. The secret of contentment is to find someone new every day and offer him a piece of yourself. It is to tell a stranger how much you admire him; to treasure every human you encounter and make him a friend.

All mankind love a lover.
Emerson

THE KOMBU KICK

One half the world cannot digest
The pleasures of the other.
Fanny Farmer

How do you thank a guy well on his way to his dotage who has all the money and sex he needs when he has gone to the plate for you? How do you tell a macho Italian who still thinks men have to be men and would never stoop to mend his jeans, iron his shirts or shed a tear, that he has saved your bank account and your future security when the guy doesn't need a single thing you have left to offer?

Remember he's Italian.

You guessed it.

YOU FEED HIM DINNER.

It was eight o'clock on the blackest Wednesday I've had since menopause. I endured a demanding book-signing event, smiling non-stop for four hours, my feet shrieking, my tummy growling and my head spinning. I raced home, pacified the dogs, finished my correspondence, condensed three loads of laundry into one tub, and galloped to a distant coffee house to take down my art exhibit before the next artist stuffed my paintings in a recycle bin. I loaded twenty-five pictures into my station wagon, battled rush-hour traffic and returned home just in time to fold the laundry and unload the car, while my chauvinist friend transformed my living room into a conference chamber.

Indeed we were both intent on our tasks, neither interfering with the other. I was doing women's work and he was doing men's.

I smoothed my disintegrating hair-do, smacked some color into my cheeks and collapsed in a waiting chair for the meeting my Italian savior had designed to help me worm out of a fraudulent contractor's agreement. I stared at the columns of figures and lists of discrepancies he had discovered, wall-eyed, while he and the contractor's wife did verbal battle that ended with me $3000 to the good. My nerves were dead, my energy level that of a bear in hibernation and my hunger pains numbed with neglect.

I looked at this heroic man's man who had done all my mediation and bargaining for me and tried to think of something I was physically capable of doing without medication to thank him. I was five years older than he, small enough to fit in his shoe and my maternal attitude is a damp blanket to anyone with anything on his mind other than a teddy bear and a kiss to make the hurt go away. The only talent I still possess that would remotely appeal to this male stereotype was my dexterity in the kitchen. I remembered my mother's adage from those long ago days when women catered to their men like we nurture our Mercedes today and I said. "Stay for dinner."

"Fine," he said. "I'll pour the wine. What are we having?"

Well, I hadn't thought about what I was going to cook. I hadn't even dealt with the breakfast dishes, for God's sake. Then I remembered that little packet of frozen green noodles made from algae in my freezer. "We are having a KOMBU KICK."

He poured himself his second glass of wine and I finished off my first. "What's that?" he asked.

I smiled. "It's a Neapolitan dish. They prepare it with delicacies extracted from the Mediterranean Sea."

"That's funny," he said. "I don't remember my mother making anything like that and she was born in Naples."

"I don't think they call it that in Italian," I said. "It's a traditional dish served at Neapolitan fiestas."

"Italians have fétes not fiestas," he said and he poured his third glass of wine.

"This is a cross-cultural dish," I said and bolted my second tumbler of la belle vino. "You drink up and I'll start sautéing."

"Good girl!" he said and that little phrase told me he had ascended to that foggy place where all of life is a heaven and everyone female a beauty queen.

He uncorked his second bottle of cabernet sauvignon. "We can knock off the zinfandel next."

"Make that singular," I said. "I am having trouble dicing. One more glass of wine and your onions will be unbraised, your garlic raw and dinner only a dream. Would you like some crackers to go with that drink?"

He shook his head, "It spoils the effect," he said. "Ready for a refill?"

"I really shouldn't!" I said and then I paused. The only thing I had to lose was my index finger. I smiled. "Just a splash. It will speed up the cooking process."

And indeed it did. I chopped onions, peppers, ginger, basil, tomatoes, cabbage, garlic and cauliflower and fried it all to a golden brown in a bubble of olive oil in less time than it takes to say *gezundheit*. I browned chicken, chopped olives, added paprika, pepper and Tabasco faster than a motorcyclist beating a red light. Then, when the pan sounded like the rhythm section of a rumba extravaganza, I dumped in those skinny little noodles I had frozen so long ago into the sizzle.

Kombu noodles are really seaweed processed to resemble pasta and this particular package came with the cockiest attitude I have seen this side of a box of macaroni. Those skinny little noodles landed in the pan and immediately leaped up like ballerinas on Spanish Fly. They soared to the ceiling grasping my vent fan for balance, dipped back into the pan and grabbed the chicken for a roller-coaster ride to my Venetian blinds. They did an arpeggio over the refrigerator, pulled three magnets from the door and dived back into the pan for a quick olive oil refresher. They paused for breath and pirouetted around the back burner, hugging my spoon holder to their hearts. They grabbed a soupçon of onion and a wad of garlic from the counter and did a deer leap into my cuisine before they descended into the dustpan next to the door.

I grabbed my spatula and reached back into childhood for the tennis skills I hadn't used for so many years and I smacked those naughty noodles back into their pan. The defied me and ricocheted into my greenhouse window, grabbed two sprigs of parsley and a bit of mint to give them the energy to execute a fancy Susie Q over to the dining room table. I leaped high into the air, waved my ladle at them like a fisherman's net and caught them in fifth position. I managed to swat their little green butts and swirl them into a complacent wad so I could push them back once more into my serving pan. I clamped on the cover and leaned against the counter to catch my breath. "Pour me a bit more of that vino," I gasped. "Or I won't have the strength to start the salad. "

"That was a spectacular performance," he said and opened a bottle of Merlot. "Where did you learn it?"

"It's a Jewish tribal dance," I said. "We always do that before the borucha."

"I'm impressed," he said. "Isadora couldn't have done better."

"Of course she couldn't," I said. "She wasn't Jewish. Have some more wine. Dinner isn't quite ready yet."

"I can't seem to see the bottle," he said. "I thought I had it here to the left of that candlestick but now I can't find it."

"By the time I toss this salad, you'll have it located," I said. "I let the lettuce do the hora with a few hard boiled eggs and a shower of red pepper. It's very unusual. You will just love this dinner. It comes with its own cabaret routine built in."

"What is that sound I hear on the stove?" he said.

I turned to view my main course struggling to lift the lid of the frying pan and do an encore. I smiled. "You are hearing a rehearsal for the main event," I said. "My noodle dish is getting itself into a good simmer so it can overwhelm the salad and win first place in your heart."

And it did.

> It's not the noodles in my life that count
> It's the life in my noodles.
> Mae West and Lynn Ruth

CHICKEN AND KOMBU CASSEROLE

Chop one large onion, two cloves of garlic and fresh basil together. Heat olive oil in a frying pan until hot and put in the mixture. Turn down the heat and let fry while you chop up zucchini, cauliflower and carrots. Add this to the pan with cut up cooked chicken, chopped olives, a fresh tomato and anything leftover that has been sitting in the refrigerator too long. Let all fry together to merge flavors until the onion is browned. and nothing looks raw. Add ½ C white wine, a teaspoon of honey mustard, pepper, grated ginger and a dash of Mrs. Dash. Cover and lock in a 250-degree oven for a warm nap until the salad is made.

BE ABSOLUTELY CERTAIN THE COVER IS ON TIGHT OR YOU WILL HAVE TO SCOOP UP YOUR DINNER FROM THE BROILER PAN.

NANCY PELLETIER

HURRY HOME

A day like any other—
Sunny, easy, busy,
My life moving in its usual circles,
And you called.

Out of the past
Your voice spoke into
This present leaving me
Shaken and confused.

No other voice,
No other name,
Could have moved me
As yours did.

And then you walked
Into my life, into my arms
And we both felt
We'd come home.

Why? Will we ever know?
I only know that for
Both of us, your call,
Our voices reliving and learning
Over the phone,
All the calls that came after,
Your presence in my home,
Pulled us together
For whatever time we
Have left to share.

So, my love,
I welcome these
Feelings, strong and unexpected,
Into this new world
That we are creating
Out of our past,
Out of this present,
And into our future.

THIS IS LOUIS WYMOND

Arriving at age 80 is a shock. Where did the time go? How much time is left? It is neither a good nor a bad feeling—just one of amazement. Looking around at this eightieth celebration, I see my children, their spouses, my grandchildren, a niece and her children—it's fine, special really. But it has a sense of ending. A life well enough lived—both bad and good with some moments of wonderful. But wait! That was July and in October there will be a jolt, a surprise far surpassing turning 80. Love is waiting in the wings.

Picture a golden October day, bright and shiny as only October can be. Picture an eighty-year-old sitting on her couch talking to a young man about a mayoral race we are working on for an upcoming election. The phone rings.

"Nancy?" A man's deep voice.

"What is this about?" My cold response to a telemarketer.

"Nancy, this is Louis Wymond."

Finally I can speak. "Louis Wymond?"

I turn to Dan. "You'll have to leave now. You'll have to let yourself out. This is an old boyfriend I haven't heard from in over sixty years."

Dutifully Dan gets up and leaves, and I turn back to the phone. All sorts of memories fill my head, of Louis as a junior and senior, the handsomest boy in our class at Anchorage High School in Kentucky, of my thrill to be his date for proms, for Ann Bullitt Brewer's ballroom dancing class, and occasionally, when he could get the car, for a date to the movies in Louisville. I struggle to get my breath. Everything has changed in some impossible to imagine way. After 64 years of no communication, Louis Wymond is back in my life.

So the courtship begins. By phone. I tell him I am busy, and I am. I am assistant director of a play at our local community theater. Thanksgiving and Christmas are coming up with all the family time that entails. When he asks to come to visit me—from Boise, Idaho, of all places—I suggest some time in January. But the phone calls come—regularly. At first, one each evening after rehearsals, and I hurry home in eager anticipation of hearing his deep voice once more. I begin to leave messages for him in case he calls.

"Hi, Louis, I'm out with friends. I'll be home around nine." Who cares what anyone else who calls thinks about this message?

Now the phone calls are coming twice a day, one morning, one evening. We talk of our children—we each have four, two girls and two boys, each six grandchildren, three girls and three boys. We tell of our divorces—mine 29 years ago, his not over yet—of our health, his sextuple bypass and diabetes, my tachycardia and atrial fib. As we talk, I continue to have this picture of him at eighteen, dark hair, dark eyes, an endearing crooked smile. For me there was always something mysterious about him, something unreachable. I tell him that I still have the gold identification bracelet that he gave me for my sixteenth birthday, the one with Nancy engraved on one side, Louis and my birthdate on the other.

And then we exchange pictures. I begin to adjust. White hair—a full head I'm glad to see—jowls, but still the same high cheekbones, lighter colored eyes than I remember. If I look very closely, I can see the boy I remembered. Boy? He's 82. What does he see with my pictures? Short hair instead of the pageboy, glasses, a little fuller of face, lines. Since that day after graduation in 1940 when I moved away with my family, we have both lived whole lifetimes. Apart.

The phone calls become more intense and the next thing I know Louis is coming to visit in mid-November. I write worrying about his expectations and mine. "Either of us could call a halt; neither of us seems to want to. Believe me, you are the *only* person I would be so curious to see. It's as if we were being allowed an unusual chance to go back all those years to remember who we were and to experience who we have turned into. My memory of our high school junior/senior relationship is one of sweetness, innocence, and pleasure in one another's company....This sudden reconnection is an adventure. And I love adventures. Apparently you do, too. And it is wonderful to have, out of the blue, this particular one. Two Leo's meeting after sixty-four years."

As I drive the two hours from Marietta, Ohio, to Columbus to pick him up, I feel ridiculous. This is folly. How could we possible be compatible after all this time? Why hadn't I just said no? In the airport I walk to the out-of-the-way place where Southwest comes in. No benches, no waiting room. A red line marks the area past which I can not go, and a dour-looking man sits on a high stool to keep watch.

"Is is all right to stand here? I'm meeting someone I haven't seen in sixty-four years and I'm not sure I'll recognize him." I know I'm babbling.

Bored, he nods his head. I wait. Soon a rush of people. The plane is in. I can hardly breathe. Some large posts support the ceiling in this area, and in a panic I get behind one. At least now I can see him first. No sign of anyone who looks like the pictures. And then—there he is. Leather jacket, baseball cap on head. A little stooped. Louis Wymond after all these years. He looks old. But he is. And so am I. He stops and speaks to the guard on the stool, and I step out from behind the post. We smile and hug a greeting and go downstairs to get his luggage.

"You know what that man said to me?" he asks. "I asked him where the waiting area was, that I was looking for someone. 'Is is someone you haven't seen in sixty-four years? She's over there behind the post.'"

For four days the courtship continues with introductions to some of my close friends, eating out, cooking for Louis. And always the talking, talking, talking. So many years to catch up on: who are children are, our grandchildren, where they live, what we'd done when we were working, trips we'd taken, our former spouses.

"I always had the feeling that your mother didn't like me," Louis says in one of our conversations.

I'm a bit taken back. His feeling is true, but should I deny it or be truthful, which we are trying to be? "You're right," I finally admit. "She thought you were too good-looking to amount to anything."

Louis laughs and waves heavenward. "Hi, Peg. Look where I am! Look who I'm with."

Later my friend Marian poses a question when I see her at the market. "Nancy, where is he staying?"

"At my house. Why?"

"Well, uh, do you think that's—well—you know?"

"Marian! I'm eighty years old. If I want a man to stay overnight at my house, I can!"

For three nights I lie in my bed as Louis lies in the guest room. I can't sleep for thinking of him being here, actually *here* under my roof after all those years. On the fourth night as we start up to bed, I blurt out. "Can we sleep together tonight?" All of my life I'd been a proper girl, someone who let the boys make the moves, never me. But now I feel that paying attention to my mother's rules simply doesn't cover this situation. I see the surprise on his face. And then he laughs.

"Nancy, Nancy, of course. I wanted to ask but I was afraid you'd be offended. The old rules just don't cover this situation, do they?"

Too soon it is time to take him back to the airport for his trip to Boise. "I'll be back," he says as he kisses me goodbye. "I'll be back in early December. Next time I'll stay longer."

Like a sixteen-year-old, I am thrilled for I very much want him to come back. I am in love, and I'm certain he is too. How does that feel at our age? Energizing! All those palpitations, the happiness that suffuses you, it is all still there. Wonderful, exciting, unbelievable.

In early December I make the trip to Columbus once more. Now we are more at ease with each other and excited to be together. We go to a local restaurant with live music, ask for "Stardust" and dance to our favorite 1940 song: "...through the mist of a memory, you wander back to me...."

That night Louis and I talk of the possibility of marriage. And before he leaves, it is decided. When his divorce is final, when he can move here, we will marry.

"I'll be back in January and the divorce should be over by then and we can talk to your minister and set a date."

We tell our children. Louis's are concerned. After all, his divorce is not yet over, and, I might add, not moving toward a conclusion very quickly. My children are dumbfounded, but generally in favor of it.

"I could think of a thousand things you might do that wouldn't surprise me, but I never thought you'd get married again!" says Mary, my eldest.

"Go for it, Mom," says son Joe, "you don't have too much time left." That's Joe. Always calling a spade a spade.

In January, Louis is back, this time for six weeks. And yes, he's at my house. My eldest granddaughter, Elizabeth, calls me to tell me how excited she is. "You're making it a lot easier for me," she says. "Jamie and I want to move in together and now we will." Hmmm. Not quite the grandmotherly example I meant to set, but what can I say?

After three weeks and a registered letter from his wife's attorney, we agree that he needs to go back to Boise to see what's happening. It isn't good. His wife wants a separation but not a divorce, and she is not cooperative. What will we do if she doesn't agree to the divorce?

In March I fly to Boise to meet his son and family. Then we drive to Spokane to meet his daughters and their families. Scary stuff. But all goes well. I like them all, and I pass the first tests. They're a bit in shock at the speed with which things are happening. But at eighty and eighty-two, how much time do we have to court?

Also in March we drive to Boulder to visit our friend Marshall and his wife Jean on the occasion of Marshall's eightieth birthday. Marshall was a classmate of ours way back in Kentucky (Class of 1940) and one of Louis's best friends. He asks Marshall to be his best man as he had been his in 1946. "Just let me know the date, and we'll be there!"

Back in Boise, we rent a trailer, load it with those belongings that Louis has salvaged from his former life, and head cross-country for Ohio. As Louis's son Ty and daughter-in-law Kristy kiss and hug us goodbye, I know this is a huge change for them to watch Louis pull up stakes. "You know," says Ty, "when I was growing up, I don't think I ever even *knew* any eighty-year-olds, and here you two are getting ready to drive clear across the United States." He shakes his head in wonder.

Louis's divorce is still not final, and while we try to make plans for a wedding, all we can do is talk. We want to be married in the Episcopal Church, St. Lukes, where I am a member. Both of us had been confirmed in the Episcopal church in Anchorage all those years ago, and I confess I attended church regularly then just to watch Louis, handsome in his red acolyte's robe, as he served at the altar. Now I ask our minister, Faith Perizzo, about making plans and find that because of our divorces, we must get permission from the bishop. Another road block.

Also before Faith can marry us, we must have three sessions of counseling! Faith could have been one of our children, and she admits that she has no idea what to tell us.

"I'll just explain church law to you, our bishop's attitude, what your choices are," she says with a shrug. "Maybe I could do my dissertation on this kind of counseling."

So we have our three sessions. Interesting but not very helpful except that we learn that getting the bishop's approval will take two months at the very least and then he might not approve. "He's ready to retire and *very* traditional," Faith says.

"How old is he?"

"Mid-seventies, I think."

Again we're older than he, but the bishop is the bishop.

From under her bangs, brown eyes serious, Faith asks, "Are you sure you two aren't going into this too quickly?"

Louis answers. "Looked at one way, from October to March is a short time, but looked at another, sixty-four years is a very long time."

Finally on March 31st comes the news that the divorce is final! We can go on with our plans. We decide to forget the bishop and have two services, one a civil ceremony on April 12th, solemnized by Judge Nuzum, the municipal judge, and later an Episcopal marriage blessing at St. Lukes with Faith presiding on May 29th, followed by a reception.

In the pouring afternoon rain, the civil ceremony is attended by family and close friends: Louis's son Ty flies from Boise to be with us, his sister Flora and her husband Gene drive from Louisville, son Joe and his girl Kitty come over from West Virginia, Faith and assorted good friends, all ten of them are seated in the jury box as we stand before the judge's bench. "Most comfortable seats in the court room," explains Judge Nuzum. And then we really are man and wife! Then it's back to the house for champagne, downtown for dinner.

The blessing service is just that—a blessing. Most of our two families are able to be there plus many, many friends. With wife Jean, Marshall comes as promised—to be best man. My two daughters, Jane and Mary, come from California and Michigan to be atttendants and Ty is there to attend his dad. My sons, Joe and Mark, are ushers, Louis's daughters, Martha and Ann from Washington state, are in charge of registering guests. A fine organist plays my favorite, the "Toccata and Fugue in D Minor," plus other Bach selections for the guests, and Maya, who has been studying opera and is the granddaughter of a dear friend, asks if she can sing for us and sing she does. We march out to the lilt of my favorite Episcopal hymn, "I sing a song of the saints of old . . . ." It was joyous all of it.

And joy follows us right to the reception. Finding a place has been difficult, but, because I am a board member, we are permitted to rent the dining room of the local retirement community, Glenwood.

"A nursing home!" Louis is aghast. "We're going to have our reception in a nursing home?"

I explain to him that it's a beautiful room, and friends invite us to dinner there where his fears are allayed.

"This is really a classy dining-room," he says with relief as we look around at the high-ceilinged room with adjoining bar, with its handsome yellow and blue color scheme, its french doors that open out to a patio. "This will be perfect. Yep, this will work."

I do not say I told you so.

Now we come into the room decorated with blue iris, white tableclothes with blue napkins. A jazz trio is holding forth; a friend sings "Stardust" for our first dance as man and wife. Wonderful food and drink; little grandchildren dancing to the jazz; big grandchildren dancing; another friend singing "It Had To Be You," a toast from our friend Marshall; a gorgeous handmade quilt hanging from daughter Martha, and a poem from all the Wymonds read by Flora, Louis's sister. A happy, happy beginning to what continues to be a wonderful life together.

Twice we've had Pansing/Wymond family reunions so that our children and grandchildren will know each other and not be just names when we talk of them. The first reunion we held at Emerald Isle, N.C. at the beach, the second one the following summer at Yellowstone near the park. Now, when Louis's granddaughter Grace has his first great-grandchild Lucy (I'd already beaten him with Sophia and Ellie from grandson Luke), both families are thrilled. Two painful divorces—one on Louis's side and one on mine—have kept both families concerned and worried. My grandchildren call Louis Granddad, his younger ones call me Nana.

Oh, yes. There is one thing more, something that I can see occasionally in the eyes of friends, but which they are too polite to ask. SEX? At eighty? Not so for Flora's teen-aged granddaughter who did blurt it out to her grandmother.

After Caitlin had met us and when she had a chance, she popped the question. "Do you suppose, Grandma, they're *getting it on*?" I imagine her horror and disdain at the idea of such a thing.

Flora's answer. "Well, I *certainly* hope so."

You'll get no more out of me.

So there it is. Love after 80. We're 85 and 87 now. A few more ailments. A little crabbiness now and then, but we are friends, we are in love, and, for our age, reasonably healthy. I am sure that our happiness contributes to our health, and we do take care of each other. Sometimes we wish that this had all happened a long time ago, but it didn't, and we're lucky that it happened at all. As I said in my letter to Louis way back in '03, I love an adventure, and this has been the adventure of a lifetime. Here's to being 90 and 92!

LAST THINGS

CAROLYN HARRIS

THE LADY IN BLACK

Late autumn sun sparkles off the hood ornament on the '57 Chevy sending dabs of gold across the black hood. Ice tinkles in his Johnny Walker as the old man pulls a folded paper towel from his shirt pocket and rubs a spot near the wipers he'd missed earlier in the day. Flying yellow leaves swirl near his head as he checks his watch then slides across the red vinyl seat and clicks the door behind him. He slips the picture of a young woman in a silver frame from the glove box. She's wearing a dress he bought for her—black like the Chevy—of some soft material that hugged her when she walked. It's been 231 days since she left him.

He lifts his glass to the smiling woman and remembers their very first time. After they cut the cake, they told their parents they were heading for Ashland, but the installment payments on the Chevy left him with just enough for dinner—so they circled back to that dinky little room they'd rented over Bender's Garage, stripped off their fancy clothes then curled up in the backseat of the new Chevy. They were going to see the USA in their Chevrolet. They'd fly past Curley's Barber Shop those half-moon taillights smiling good bye. He touches her face. Four kids and five years later, they were lucky to see two dimes the day before payday.

Wind bumps the wing window. He rides through the memories and wonders again what was up that time she thought he was slipping around with Ruby Dean and took the kids and moved in with her sister. Even after she came back home, he'd catch her sniffling around when she didn't think he was watching. Then, she starved herself, trying to get back into those jeans she wore in high school—when she knew he always liked a woman with a little meat on her bones. That's one of the things he's going to get straightened out next time he sees her.

He sips the Johnny Walker and watches her rose garden drink in the last sunshine of the day. Maybe she needed him to spend more time with her—but that was when he was working the night shift at Kelly's Mill and delivering milk four days a week to make the payments on her station wagon.

Two tangled leaves skid across the windshield. He closes his eyes remembering how the miles went by. When they got the new house, they kept the Chevy in the barn. They'd tell the kids they were going out, then park the station wagon down by her mom's and sneak back and eat chocolates and drink wine in the back seat of the Chevy. They'd creep up to the house in the dark every once in a while just to make sure the kids weren't tearing the house down. He still remembers the smell of her hair, damp from a shower. He rubs his hand across the red vinyl seat and smiles. Sometimes they'd even make out a little, squeezed in back there, but it never went all the way. By then, neither one of them could get in their high school jeans, and they were so tired from remodeling that extra room for the kids they usually fell asleep. He taps the steering wheel as he remembers the night her mom rapped on the Chevy window and told them all the kids were down at her house and Jaimie wanted to call the state police because somebody had kidnapped his parents.

The last of the litter, Jaimie always was a wild one. He rubs his sore knee and watches the grass shiver. When Jaimie died, he went to town to drink—just couldn't stand to be around the house. He blamed himself for letting him buy that damn Ford. He just couldn't say, "Don't race that thing," when he was the one who taught Jamie to drive. A drop slides down his glass. He swipes it away with his thumb, remembering how she pulled him into the back seat of their Chevy and let him cry. He thinks that was probably the first time he really bawled like a baby. He's getting pretty good at it now. "Say hello to Jaimie. We haven't talked for a while," he tells the silent picture.

A sparrow teeters on the hood ornament then disappears in a swirl of leaves, and for a moment he wonders if it was her. It's funny how she borrows a body sometimes just to remind him to get a haircut or water her roses.

He checks his watch. It's time to warm his TV dinner. He runs his finger around the silver frame and winks at the smiling woman. "You said you'd wait for me and find a place for the two of us. Just make sure it's big enough—'cause I'm bringing our '57 Chevy."

STEPHANIE FEUER

SOMEBODY TO LOVE
Excerpts

The following are two excerpts from, "Somebody to Love," a novel (as yet unpublished) set in the tumultuous spring of 1968. When the love affair between two nursing home residents becomes the subject of a newspaper expose, seventeen year-old Hannah Cooper sets out to refute the story to save the reputation of the old age home her father runs and exposes the many facets of love—the sweetness of the first, the depth of the father-daughter bond and the surprising lightness of one last fling. The two excerpts show the developing relationship between the two nursing home residents.

In this excerpt Margaret, a long time-resident of the nursing home (called The Place) befriends a new resident, Herman Steiner, a former photographer:

A few days after the welcome dinner for Herman Steiner, a stroke victim, Margaret went up to the third floor and brought Mr. Steiner a copy of *The Times*. She hadn't finished reading it, but figured he might nap and she could get it back then. Mr. Steiner was sitting by himself, not watching the TV, in the corner of the light green common room, under the framed bright yellow Marimekko fabric flower.

"I could tell you weren't much interested in *The Herald*. May I sit down?" Margaret asked, *Times* in hand, in reference to their conversation at his welcome dinner. Mr. Steiner gestured to the seat next to him and with his good hand, snatched the second section of the paper from her. She unfolded the front page and started reading aloud.

"Big news this morning. Johnson says he won't run," she said neutrally, hoping to elicit an opinion. Mr. Steiner responded with a nod. Margaret turned the page.

"Bet that means that Humphrey will run," she continued, shaking her long white mane of hair. Mr. Steiner half shrugged, the gesture, though small, was more labored than disinterested.

In a couple of minutes Margaret tried again, carefully folding the paper first lengthwise then in half to show a picture. It was of Paris, a view of protesters from a distance. In the bottom of the frame, a single protester was heading toward the crowd, shoulders forward, captured in a quick, determined walk.

"An extraordinary photo," she said, "makes you feel like you're walking right into the action."

Mr. Steiner scrutinized it, and her. He said nothing. But his face telegraphed that something resonated deeply. Margaret tried to bring it out of him.

"I think that boy has courage," she said pointing to the protester in the photo. "Pahr-ee," she continued in a not bad French accent, "it even sounds heavenly. Ever been there?"

Mr. Steiner looked back at her long and hard. He moved his body slightly forward, then back, a full body nod, the motion telling Margaret it was a place he had fully experienced. He leaned in towards her, his lips parted. Mr. Steiner did not say a word.

Each day that week, Margaret again brought her carefully folded newspaper to the third floor lounge. Mr. Steiner would gesture for her to sit down and Margaret would talk about the headlines, often looking up and into his deep, brown eyes. Mr. Steiner did not talk.

"You can get a paper here, you know," she said to him at the end of the week, although she was glad he had not yet made that effort. He nodded in affirmation, his motion stronger and surer than the previous day, letting her know that he was at least accepting of her company, perhaps even welcoming it.

Emboldened, Margaret offered, "Join me for lunch. You don't have to eat in your room. Sit at my table—the nurses call us the live wires. You'll hear some good stories. Wait 'til Mrs. G gets going. Or Solly, he's a regular history scholar."

Herman Steiner lowered his head and said nothing. Then he looked away, glancing at the residents in wheelchairs watching the TV. Margaret let the silence sit a minute, thick and loaded. Time at The Place was measured against a different clock. Simple everyday tasks could be slow and savored when there was incremental progress, while catastrophes, happened quickly and frequently. With an uncertain ending ever looming, the pace of relationships was akilter, accelerated and intensified.

"What do you say? Tomorrow, maybe?" she said, lightly touching him on his arm.

Mr. Steiner still said nothing. His chin sunk deeper towards his chest. Margaret waited. All week she'd been making an effort and now she was giving him plenty of time to summon some words, or even a simple gesture of thanks. But Mr. Steiner receded, lost in himself, wallowing.

Margaret was stung by his lack of effort, his seeming lack of response to her. "It's not like you're the first person who has had a stroke," she said.

He looked up at her, as if he was shocked at her boldness and change of tone. His face reddened from shame.

"You strike me as a man who had good manners." She let her words sink in for a second before she continued, "Do you want to be locked inside yourself forever? Tell me, did you spend your life around people?"

His eyes widened in a mix of fear and gratitude. With a slight nod of his head, he mouthed "yes."

"Did you have a lot of friends, talk about ideas and music and people you knew?" And then she softened, "Did you spend a lot of time in Paris?"

Tears filled his eyes. His mouth contorted, the left side refusing to hold a shape. In more a hiss than a whisper, he uttered "Yes. Oh g-g-God, yes."

He reached his hand to her. She stroked it. Quiet for a minute, they sat, Mr. Steiner averting his eyes like a vulnerable, guilty little boy. His face quivered. His cheeks puffed and reddened from the effort of his forced words. He bent forward and balled up his right hand. His knuckles were white from tension and frustration. But it was too hard, and he let out a long, sad breath and said nothing.

Margaret's voice turned motherly as she said, "You'll never be what you were. But you don't have to be like this either. You can try. You can learn to adjust. Get them to pay for physical therapy. You'll get better with time. It's your money isn't it? Talk to Mr. Cooper. Or you'll crumble from loneliness or turn hard and sour."

She got up and walked across the room to the magazine rack filled with old issues of *Life*, *Esquire* and *Family Circle*. She picked up a big stack. Margaret sat down next to his good side and moved her chair closer to him. She opened a magazine, spread it across his legs and pointed to the pictures.

"So who are you, Mr. Steiner? Show me who you are."

Later that spring, Steiner's condition has improved and their relationship has deepened.

Herman greeted Margaret with a wave of his left hand as she entered his room. As he did so, the movement felt fluid, his bad hand lighter somehow. He looked at his hands, and did as Nurse Claire had instructed, visualizing a connection, a set of train tracks she'd said, going from his brain to his fingers. Then send the message down those tracks, she'd told him. Movement on his affected side would no longer be automatic. There had to be intent. He could will his movements if he could really focus his attention, she'd told him at one of their recent sessions.

He shut out everything and thought only of bending the fingers of his left hand. For the first time in weeks, he was able to coax some movement from them. He looked at them like a baby does its feet, as if first understanding their connection to him. He looked up at Margaret and clumsily waved his hand.

Margaret smiled broadly and her eyes met his. She touched her fingers to her lips and threw him a kiss. He moved his left hand towards his lips in a shaky but accurate movement. He held his lips on his fingers for a very long second, holding her gaze. He completed the gesture, almost gracefully opening his palm to her, throwing her a kiss.

"The medicine is working," she exclaimed, moved by this deep and simple gesture.

"And Claire," he said more clearly than he had been able to since he came to The Place.

Heartened by the clarity of his words, and the welcome conversation, he continued, "Glad you're here." With his right hand he pointed to the room around him. "Sick of the plain wh-walls. Need some beauty."

Margaret sat down carefully at the side of the bed. He stroked her arm and they sat quietly. He reached out his left hand and held her. "Better," he said,

With his right hand he undid the bobby pins in her hair, slowly, methodically. He tussled a section of hair on the side to let it loose. Margaret shook her head and the rest of it flowed down dramatically. He wound a circle of hair around his finger. She leaned into him, their checks touching. She smoothed her hair across his face. He closed his eyes and sighed. With his good right hand he stroked her back.

"Do you have much pain?" he asked her after a moment.

She moved his hand to where it hurt, her upper gut, and he rubbed it for a while, watching the deep lines in her face soften.

After a few moments, Herman turned to Margaret determinedly.

"My camera," he said, pointing to the bottom dresser drawer. She opened the drawer and carefully removed his Leica from its case.

He gestured for Margaret to sit in the guest chair and fiddled with the camera's dials.

"Look at me."

Margaret looked at him. His hands shook from weakness and emotion. He looked over the camera to catch her eye, drawing her gaze to the lens. He looked back down through the lens, sucked in his breath and clicked the shutter.

"Damn," he said, knowing that the camera shook as the shutter released.

Margaret rearranged her hair so it all hung on one side. "This is better, anyway."

He looked up at her. "Mmm."

The way he looked at her made her feel attractive. He held her glance, feeling his old photographic instincts kick in as he took several shots.

With effort he pulled himself up and out of bed and walked over to where she sat. He carefully balanced the camera as he took her in his arms. He leaned his left side against the wall for balance and kissed her, his mouth not doing quite what he willed, but it felt magnificent, holding her, safe and warm.

He moved her hair about her face and fumbled with one of her shirt buttons. Margaret unbuttoned the top ones as he took some of the lipstick from her lips and smudged it on each of her cheeks. From the side of the bed he took some Vaseline and rubbed it on her eyelashes, put some on her lips and a tiny dot on the high part of her cheekbones. He positioned her so the light just hit her cheek, the reflection illuminating her face. He stood back and looked.

Margaret felt a tingle through her body. He reached over with his good hand and tugged at her bra. She helped him unfasten it. She felt her nipple harden. Instinctively her hand grasped the fabric of her dress to cover herself. He placed his hand on hers, and she gave in to his insistence. As he spread her blouse open, he revealed her alabaster chest; a line of scars crossed one side where her breast had been. He traced the line gently. To his photographer's eyes her mastectomy scar was a thing of beauty. As his hand grazed it over and over again, Margaret twitched. He placed the camera in her lap, and with his good right hand teased her remaining nipple between his thumb and index finger. She moaned softly.

"Hold that feeling," he said as he recaptured his camera and positioned himself against the dresser, catching her ecstasy at a side angle. He pictured how it would look in the frame, adjusted his angle and took several more shots. Her expression turned daring and a flush was rising in her cheeks. Herman clicked the shutter again, finding it harder to hold the camera steady as his legs quivered.

As he fired off the last shot, they heard a knock at the door.

"Mr. Steiner. Medicine." It was Nurse Claire.

Margaret fumbled with her buttons. Herman frantically pointed to her bra. She picked it up from where it had fallen on the floor.

"Mr. Steiner? Are you OK?"

"Just a minute," Herman replied, clearly and forcefully.

Margaret couldn't help but giggle as she put the bra on the chair and sat on it.

Herman opened the door.

Nurse Claire glanced over at the empty bed. "I see you're up and around," then as she caught sight of Margaret, disheveled and sitting awkwardly in the guest chair, she added, "And you've had a bit of medicine, too."

MARSHA MATHEWS

PREPARATION

Rocky Face, Georgia

Her mouth bends. Her back twists.
She struggles to sit up.

"Yes, ma'am, let us help you."
We carry her to her bath.

Lifting her is like lifting lavender.
Her flannel gown opens

to breasts, ivory magnolias.
Through steam,

she sets aside ninety years of dignity,
lets us spray her down,

sponge her back.
"Ooh, that feels good, so good."

To touch her skin is to touch angels' wings.
She forgets about Hospice,

remembers her husband, dead forty years,
his body heat.

"Ooh. Do that again. Again."
Her back bends, Odysseus's bow.

THE WOMAN WHO ISN'T HIS WIFE

says, too loud, words
that should be whispered,

"Doc says he ain't got much time."

The patient's startled eyes
rise up like axes
before shutting down.
His body pulls air
one more time.

Machines gurgle.

His hand jerks.

Now the loud, labored breathing,
is hers.

"We met at the diner in Norton,
Sat on silver stools that twirled
while we drank Cherry Coke-a-Colas.
Horses clopped the streets. Those days
men, their faces black with coal, walked
about, chewing tobacco. Had to make
a law against spitting on the sidewalk.

Years later, the booze got him.

Tried so hard to change him.
Tried so hard to love him.
Tried so hard to leave him."

Nurses buzz doctors.
Blue masks, swift moves.

The woman who is not
supposed to be here
handkerchiefs his brow

one last time
slips out
before the legal wife slips in.

MARTIN LINDAUER

AN ANONYMOUS DEATH

For nearly seven years, on Friday afternoons, I've been a "Friendly Visitor" at the Home. My specialty, if you could call it that, was spending time with residents who had no relatives or friends to visit them. I'd spend a few minutes with a frail senior chatting, neatening up a cluttered tabletop, or reading a newspaper aloud. Paula, though, received most of my attention.

She had suffered a stroke and could not speak, walk, or use her left hand. She was bedridden, too, and if that wasn't enough, she was blind as well.

Her hearing was fine, though. I'd stand at her open door, knock, and ask (unnecessarily), "Anyone home?" She'd invite me in with a grunt and perhaps a twinkle in her eye.

Typically, I'd sit down next to her bed, summarize the day's headlines (excluding murders, wars, and other bad news), and watch her eyes. If I caught a glimmer of interest, I'd say a little more until she looked away. "Enough" the movement told me. It didn't take long to exhaust the newspaper's good news.

When that happened, I shifted to a short check-list. "How was lunch today?" Paula can't swallow and eats only strained baby food. A guttural response was a positive sign, a wave of the hand negative. Next I might ask about the sound on the TV. She can't see the picture, of course, but she could listen, and she liked soap operas.

Aids constantly bustled in and out during my stay, bringing Paula new linen, fresh towels, or a juice to sip through a straw. Business-like, the aids would brusquely nod at me but say nothing to Paula. They knew there was no point trying to engage her in even a brief exchange.

I ignored the interruptions and continued to chatter, alert for any signs of interest. I spoke of ordinary things, everyday matters, the kinds of subjects friends normally shared. "Hasn't it been unusually cool this summer?" No response. "Do you know what bananas cost at Safeway this week?" Paula stared unseeingly ahead. I'd tell her what I had for lunch that day. She'd stop me with a half-wave of a thin and blue-veined hand and emit a throaty rumble.

I'd rummage through my memory searching for some tidbit worth telling her about. I scanned the room for conversational inspiration. But there were no photos, plants, or nick-knacks on the walls or shelves, no residue from her past. Why expect a blind person to be surrounded by visual objects?

At a loss of what to talk about, I might fall back on describing the traffic that had delayed my arrival at the Home (true or not). One time Paula lifted her chin. A sign of interest? Encouraged, I plowed ahead. "Uh, did you ever own a car? Mm, have you taken long trips?" She nodded. Wow! Wasn't such a dumb question after all. I quickly followed-up. "Have you seen much of the United States?" She dipped her head. Was that a yes? I pushed ahead, excited by my small success. "Have you ever traveled to Europe? Paris?" She lay motionless as I listed other cities until I ran out of names of capitols I could remember.

I sighed and tried another tack. "Did you ever fly? Take a cruise?" Her chin sinks lower with each question. I've taken a barren path and lost her.

I changed subjects abruptly but she never objected. Following the travel quiz, for example, I told her how much money was in the lottery pool that week. She turned her head. Was there some interest? "Uh, did you ever gamble?" She shook her head. Was that a no?

Uncertain, I dropped the subject and babbled on about the latest styles in women's shoes. She growled and fluttered a hand. "Move on," her slumped shoulders signaled. I'm grateful she changed the subject. What do I know of women's fashions?

"I picked up a free ticket for the ballet at the Senior Center," I once told her. Her face lit up and I seized the clue. "Uh, did you ever dance as a kid?"

Out of the corner of my eye I spotted the outline of Paula's spindly legs under the flimsy coverlet. I grimaced. How dumb, asking about dancing when she can't walk. Embarrassed, I'm unsure of how to extract myself.

I'm rescued by the sound of music on the TV. "Did you ever play the piano?" Another gaff, I realize, when I catch sight of her arthritically arched fingers. I get up and switch channels on the TV and stumble onto a cooking class. "Do you like to cook?" A blank look is the answer. I mumbled something about changes in the Social Security cost-of-living index.

A social worker, knowing of my struggles to fill time with Paula, offered to let me read her file, but I refused. I wasn't comfortable about prying into Paula's personal life. No friend would do that, not a real one. Anyway, how much conversational chitchat could I pick up from medical reports?

At a loss of what to say one week, I pulled out a black-and-white snapshot from my wallet. "You can't see what I'm holding, Paula, but it's a picture of my daughter when she was a baby." Paula stared unseeingly in my direction, slowly raised her only working hand up to the angular planes of her gaunt face, gently laid a palm against a cheek crevassed with wrinkles, closed trembling lids over watery eyes, and rocked back and forth. What do those gestures mean? I wondered. Have I said something stupid?

Tentatively, I concluded that Paula once had a child, but it had died as an infant. Where do I to go with this? I asked myself. Should I ask, "Was your child a boy or girl? What happened to your husband?" I didn't grill her, though. What if my initial interpretation was wrong?

There were other questions I might have asked but never did. "Are you lonely? How do you overcome feelings of despair, the emptiness of time, the meaninglessness of each day?" Some answers cannot be communicated by mime.

Last Friday, as usual, I signed in at the volunteer office and scanned the "In Memoriam" board. Who had died since my last visit? I dreaded the possibility of walking into the room of one of my regulars, ready to give a cheery greeting, only to find the bed stripped, its metal under girding exposed, a signal that the present occupant was deceased and the room was ready for the next person on the waiting list.

At I entered Paula's wing of the building the charge nurse intercepted me. "Paula is in a coma. Swallowing has become impossible but she refused to be fed intravenously. She wants to die." Morphine was being administered, I was told, until Paula slept into death.

I sat at Paula's bedside, my eyes damp, and held her limp hand. What words can acknowledge the end of a difficult life? I asked myself. I left the room and borrowed a copy of the *Bible* from the Home's library and began to read *Ecclesiastes* aloud.

Halfway through, I took a break and wondered if there might be a relative who lived too far away to visit Paula. Perhaps an old friend, too fragile to make the trip. Someone should be notified of Paula's condition.

I opened the single drawer of Paula's night table, hoping I might find a letter with a name and address I could call. I thumbed through old menus, last month's schedule of events, and outdated notices from the Home. Buried in a loose pile of charitable requests I uncovered an engraved card with the Presidential Seal. Wow! A note from the White House signed by John Kennedy honoring Paula's 100th birthday.

I smiled. Why didn't I find this before? *That* would have been something to talk about.

Me

AUTHORS

Jill C. Alt published her first poem in a now-defunct literary magazine called *Asterisk* in 1956. This was followed by a fifty-year hush until the poetry bug bit again in 2001. Most likely it had something to do with the Writer's Center in Bethesda, Maryland, which abounds in poetry workshops and gives poets both the encouragement and criticism so necessary for growth. The poet is presently a government lawyer, and has been an actress, painter, mother, wife, and it's not over yet.

Lois Barr has taught Spanish language and literature for thirty-six years. She started out with a bike and two pairs of jeans as a teaching assistant at the University of Kentucky. She ended up tenured in a suit and a Ford Escape at Lake Forest College. Her poems and essays have appeared in *Collage*, *East on Central* and *94 Creations*.

William Borden's book-length poem *Eurydice's Song* was published by Bayeux Arts, Calgary, and St. Andrew's Press, Laurinberg, NC. His poems have appeared in over 100 magazines and anthologies and in a chapbook, *Slow Step and Dance*. His novel *Dancing with Bears* is forthcoming from Livingston Press. His novel *Superstoe* was reissued by Orloff Press. The film adaptation of his play *The Last Prostitute* was shown on Lifetime Television.

Regina Murray Brault has published her poetry in approximately 85 different magazines, anthologies, and chapbooks including: *Ancient Paths Literary Magazine*, *Anthology of New England Writers*, *Comstock Review*, *Grandmother Earth*, *Hartford Courant*, *Mothers and Daughters* (June Cotner Anthology), *Karamu*, *Mennonite*, *Northwoods Journal*, *Poet Magazine*, and *State Street Review*. Regina is also the recipient of more than 240 poetry awards including first place in the 2007 Euphoria, and Skysaje Enterprises Poetry Competitions.

Patricia Brodie is a clinical social worker with a private psychotherapy practice in Concord, MA. Her poems have appeared in *The Comstock Review, The Lyric, California Quarterly, Raintown Review, The Pedestal, Phoebe* and many other journals as well as many anthologies. She has won several awards in poetry contests and her chapbook *The American Wives Club* (Ibbetson Street Press) was published in 2006.

Anna Chance has been writing prose and poetry since 1994, having retired from a forty-year nursing career. Ranching and city life have shaped her short stories and poems published in several mid-western literary journals as well as a weekly health column. Home care for a family member consumes much time. Children's stories and novella are awaiting a willing editor. Seventy is a delightful age.

Joan Dobbie, M.F.A., teaches poetry and yoga in Eugene, Oregon, where she lives. Most recently, her poem "Ash" took Second Place in an Oregon State Poetry Association contest (Fall 2006) and appeared in their anthology; "Remembering" received an honorable mention in their Traditional Verse category (Fall 2005); and "How I Came to Be on Earth" appeared in DONA NOBIS PACEM (Grant Us Peace), April 2006. Enjoy her website: <joandobbie.blogspot.com>

Juditha Dowd divides her time between poetry and prose. Her work has appeared in many print and online journals and anthologies, including *Florida Review, California Quarterly, Perigee, Earth's Daughters* and *AARP Magazine*. Finishing Line Press published a chapbook, *The Weathermancer*, in 2006. She was recently awarded fellowships by the Geraldine R. Dodge Foundation, Virginia Center for the Creative Arts and Vermont Studio Center. Dowd is completing a book-length manuscript of poetry and has recently begun a second novel.

Marilynn Dunham lives in Northern California. Her dream was to live by the sea with Grandma Ocean as her Muse, and write her stories. She is now 76 and that dream has come true. Her educational background is Swiss cheese; with holes where college degrees and teaching careers might be, but no matter where she lived or which child she tended she always found a creative writing class.

Stephanie Feuer is a New York writer whose work has appeared in publications including *The New York Times, The New York Daily News, The Boston Herald, The Mom Egg* and the anthology, *Democrat Soul*. She is a creative non-fiction editor for the literary journal *Conclave*.

Bernice M. Fisher has published her short stories in *The Young Judean* and *Ariston*. Three of her non-fiction memoirs appeared in *Ramsey County History*. She has also published articles in *The Catholic Digest, The Minneapolis Star-Tribune*, and written a weekly column for *The Pine City Pioneer*. She is a native of St. Paul, Minnesota.

Maureen Tolman Flannery, having thrived in a forty-five-year love adventure, has alchemized most aspects of it into poetry. She and her actor husband, Dan, have been blessed with four fascinating children. Her poems have appeared in *Atlanta Review, Pedestal, Calyx, North American Review* and hundreds of other journals and anthologies. Her books are *A Fine Line, Secret of the Rising Up, Ancestors in the Landscape, Remembered into Life,* and *Knowing Stones*.

Emilie George is an Albanian-American, retired French teacher, a singer/songwriter who performs international folk songs. Three albums recorded for Folkways are now available in the Smithsonian Catalog. Recent CD with Stefan George, "My Father's Mansion: Hands Around the World with International Songs." Poetry published in: *The Sow's Ear, Lifeboat: A Journal of Memoir, American Recorder,* and *Meridian Anthology of Contemporary Poetry*.

Maralee Gerke lives in Madras, Oregon. She grew up on a farm in the Willamette Valley but has lived in Central Oregon for over 30 years. Her poems reflect experiences from both sides of Oregon. She has poetry published in *Calyx, Windfall, Anthology, Cascade Reader, Tiger's Eye* and many other small journals. In 2003 she published her first chapbook of poems called *Looking Back, Facing Forward*; her second book, *Like Pearls on My Tongue,* was published in 2006.

Ann Goethe lives in Virginia on a small peninsula overlooking the ancient New River. Her novel, *Midnight Lemonade*, was a Finalist for the Barnes and Noble "Discovery Prize" and was published in Germany, Sweden, Israel and Korea. She is a published playwright; her poems, essays and short stories have appeared in journals such as *The Southern Review, The Crescent Review, The New Orleans Review, Inkwell,* and *Clare.*

Myrna Goodman is a ceramic artist, poet, and co-editor/publisher of *Toadlily Press.* She writes on and off the clay. Her artwork has been shown recently at the Katonah Museum of Art, and her poems have been published in many journals including *The Cortland Review, Confrontation* and *Karamu.* Her chapbook, *Some Assembly Required*, was published in *Desire Path* in 2005. She lives, with her husband of 52 years, in Chappaqua, NY.

Martha Deborah Hall's poems appear in national journals including, *Bellowing Ark, Common Ground Review, Las Cruces, Old Red Kimono, Seldom Nocturne, Shemom, Tale Spinners, The Poet's Touchstone, Watch the Eye,* and in the Nashua NH Poets Unbound anthology, *Poems from the Cranberry Room.* She is the winner of the 2005 John and Mirium Morris Chapbook contest. She has degrees from Ohio Wesleyan and Columbia University and is President of Amherst Historical Properties Real Estate in New Hampshire.

Carolyn Harris lives in the Cascade Mountains with her husband, Dave, and too many cats. She is a member of the Squaw Valley Community of Writers. She blogs at <http://blog.seattlepi.nwsource.com/lynscircle/> and <http://travelingnewzealand.blogspot.com>. Her articles have appeared in travel and sailing magazines, and her book *RV in NZ: How to Spend Your Winters South in New Zealand* can be seen at <www.rvinnz.com>. *Wednesday's Child,* a novel set in a northern California logging camp, is looking for a home.

Grey Held is a graduate of the Massachusetts Institute of Technology and a recipient of a National Endowment for the Arts Fellowship in Poetry. His poems have been included in anthologies, including *Mercy of Tides, Familiar,* and *O Taste and See.* He lives with his wife, a costume designer, in Newton, MA, where they have raised their two children, and manages an international team of research analysts at a high-tech consulting firm.

Roxanne Hoffman, a former Wall Street banker, now answers a patient hotline for a major New York home health care provider. Her poetry is anthologized in *The Bandana Republic: A Literary Anthology By Gang Members And Their Affiliates* (Soft Skull Press) and can be heard during the independent film, "Love & The Vampire," directed by David Gold. She and her husband own the small press, Poets Wear Prada.

Phyllis Langton, PhD, RN, is Professor Emerita, George Washington University, Washington, DC. Her specialty fields include: Health and Illness, Health Policy, and Management. She was a recent Fellow at the Robert M. MacNamara Foundation in Maine and the Hambidge Center for the Creative Arts in Georgia. Her essays are from her memoir in progress, *Living Well in the Face of Death.*

Martin Lindauer has written short fiction, essays, and memoirs for *Ha!, The Jewish Magazine, Oracle, Poetica, Slab*, and others. He is a retired professor of psychology who has published widely on psychology and the arts, including *The Psychological Study of Literature* (1975, Nelson-Hall) and *Aging, Creativity, and Art* (2003, Springer). He is currently completing a scholarly monograph on the psychological relevance of literary content.

Christina Lovin is the author of *What We Burned for Warmth* and *Little Fires*. An award-winning writer, her work has been widely published. Named Emerging Poet by 2007 Southern Women Writers' Conference, she has been residency fellow at Vermont Studio Center, Virginia Center for the Creative Arts, and Footpaths House in the Azores. Her work has been recognized by Kentucky Foundation for Women and Kentucky Arts Council.

Marsha Mathews teaches writing at Dalton State College in Georgia. She has published poetry in numerous literary magazines, including *Apalachee Quarterly, Greensboro Review, Kansas Quarterly,* and *Pembroke*. Her poem "Grasshopper" appears in the online teaching text, *In the Heydays of His Eyes* <www.heydays.ws>. The poems presented in *Love After 70* are from her chapbook *A Congregation Fans a Mountainous Tale*. Marsha is seeking an agent for her novel *Blood Feather.*

Janice H. Mikesell has published her poetry in *Visions International, R-KV-RY, South Dakota Review, Kalliope, Midwest Quarterly,* and *Mid-American Review.*

Lynn Ruth Miller's story collections *Thoughts While Walking the Dog* and *More Thoughts While Walking the Dog* were published in 2001. Her two novels are *Starving Hearts* published May, 2000 and *The Late Bloomer* published in 2005 and are available on her website www.lynnruthmiller.com and Amazon.com. Her storytelling shows have been presented in San Francisco, Fresno and at the Edinburgh Festival Fringe. Her work has appeared in over 300 publications.

Angela Conti Molgaard has published in variety of publications worldwide including *The South China Morning Post, Institutional Investor, Scanorama, Penthouse, Jyllands Posten, Dance Teacher Now, Tertulia Magazine, Schuylkill Valley Journal* and anthologies—*Swaying* and *Cupid's Wild Arrows.* She currently resides in Seattle, Washington.

Mary O'Dell, founder and president of Green River Writers, Inc., lives in Louisville, Kentucky and has been writing poetry for most of her life. Her collections *Poems for the Man Who Weighs Light* and *Living in the Body* were published by Mellen Poetry Press, and a chapbook, *The Dangerous Man*, was accepted by Finishing Line Press. She has had work in such journals as *Passager Poetry Journal, The Sow's Ear, Passages North, The Roanoke Review* and *The Louisville Review.*

Carl Palmer, 2008 nominee for the Pushcart Prize, is the author of *Telling Stories, Memory Moments* and *Family Matters,* books of flash fiction and poetry he has performed at open mikes in the Puget Sound region of the Pacific Northwest. <www.myspace.com/carl_papa_palmer>

Julie Preis has returned to writing poetry not very long ago after a hiatus of several decades. Her poetry has been published online in the *Innisfree Poetry Journal* and *Best Poem.* She lives in Silver Spring, MD, and works for AARP.

Joyce Richardson is the author of an Appalachian novel, *On Sunday Creek* and a tarot chapbook, *The Reader*. Her short stories and poems have been published in *Riverwind, Appalachian Heritage, Voices International, The Writer, Pinesong,* and *AAUW Journal,* among others. She lives and writes in Athens, Ohio, where she cohabits with her writer husband, Phil.

Phil Richardson is retired from Ohio University in Athens, Ohio. He met his wife there in a creative writing class and they both continue to write. He publishes genre fiction, flash fiction, and literary fiction. He is currently working on a novel. His work has appeared in *Elf: Eclectic Literary Forum, Fantasy, Folklore and Fairytales, Northwoods Review, The Storyteller, Cafe Irreal, Digitalis Obscura, Big Pulp, Muzzle Flash,* and *Writing On Walls Anthology.*

Elisavietta Ritchie's 15 books include *Real Toads; Awaiting Permission to Land; Spirit of the Walrus; Arc of the Storm; Elegy for the Other Woman; Tightening The Circle Over Eel Country; Raking The Snow; In Haste I Write You This Note; Flying Time.* Editor of *The Dolphin's Arc: Endangered Creatures of the Sea,* and others, her work is widely published, translated and anthologized. Ex-president for poetry, then fiction, Washington Writers' Publishing House.

Frank Salvidio's poems have won First Prize, High Distinction and Honorable Mention awards in various contests. A retired college professor, he is the author of several books: *Between Troy & Florence* (original poems and translations), *Sappho Says* (translations of poems and fragments of Sappho of Lesbos), and translations of Dante's *Vita Nuova* and, most recently, Dante's *Inferno.*

Cynthia Sample holds a Ph.D. in business from University of Texas at Dallas, and M.F.A. from Vermont College. Active in church and community, she presents reviews to area book clubs. In summer of 2007, she was one of four emerging writers to present her work at the WordSpace Literary Festival. Her stories have appeared in *Dreams & Visions* and *Between the Lines.* She lives in Dallas, Texas, with her husband.

Wayne Scheer retired after twenty five-years of teaching writing and literature in college to follow his own advice and write. He has been nominated for a Pushcart Prize and a Best of the Net. His stories, essays and poems have appeared in print and online in such publications as *The Christian Science Monitor, Notre Dame Magazine, Pedestal Magazine, flashquake, Eclectica* and *River Walk Journal.* Wayne lives with his wife in Atlanta.

Ada Jill Schneider, winner of the National Galway Kinnell Poetry Prize, is the author of *Behind the Pictures I Hang* (Spinner Publications 2007), *The Museum of My Mother* (Gratlau Press 1996) and *Fine Lines and Other Wrinkles* (Gratlau Press 1993). She reviews poetry books for *Midstream* magazine and directs "The Pleasure of Poetry," a program she founded at the Somerset Public Library in Massachusetts. At the age of sixty-six, Ada received her MFA in Writing at Vermont College.

Alexandrina Sergio's poems have recently appeared or are forthcoming in *Long River Run, Caduceus, Connecticut River Review* and *Wisdom of Our Mothers* (Familia Books). Her work has been performed by a professional stage company, was awarded an honorable mention by the National Federation of State Poetry Societies and received first place in a 2007 statewide Connecticut Senior Poetry Contest. Performing poetry in public is Sandy's idea of fun.

Lucille Gang Shulklapper, a workshop leader for the Florida Center for the Book, has won awards and competitions. Her work has been anthologized and appears in many publications as well as in her four poetry chapbooks, *What You Cannot Have; The Substance of Sunlight; Godd, It's Not Hollywood;* and *In the Tunnel.*

Claudette Mork Sigg has published poetry in *Natural Bridge, the Atlanta Review, The Journal of the American Medical Association, Colere, Pinyon, Into the Teeth of the Wind,* and *Earth's Daughters,* as well as in the anthologies, *Sierra Songs & Descents, Rough Places Plain: Poems of the Mountains,* Chapman and Strasser's *75 Poems on Retirement,* and *Illness & Grace / Terror & Transformation.*

Ruth Margolin Silin, former Director of Development at a pediatric hospital and a graduate of Northeastern University where she returned as an adult student, has been writing intermittently over the years. Now retired, she has more time to observe, reflect, and obsessively revise the words that take her on a meandering journey. Her poetry focuses on love, loss, and the incidentals of life which she views with a combination of angst and humor. Her poems have appeared in *Ibbetson Street, Parnassus, Hidden Oak, Pralaton, Hazmat* and other publications.

Roger B. Smith was born in Rochester, New York, in 1939. He grew up on a fruit and dairy farm in rural Wayne County. He studied painting at The Art Student's League in New York, and the San Francisco Art Institute. His poems and stories have appeared in *Beginnings Magazine, State Street Press, Tiger's Eye Journal,* and *The Sun Magazine.* Smith lives in the foothills of the Adirondack Mountains and works with Americorps-VISTA at The Underground Café, a teen drop-in center in Utica, New York.

Paul Sohar emerged from his private garden of poetry while serving his apprenticeship as a translator of contemporary Hungarian prose and poetry. Early retirement from a drug company research lab also helped him turn out nine books of translations before he finally had a volume of his own poetry *Homing Poems* (Iniquity Press, 2005). His magazine credits include *Chiron, Kenyon Review, Main Street Rag, Pedestal, Poem, Poesy, Rattle,* etc.

Anna Steegmann, born in Germany, is a bilingual writer and translator who lives in New York City and teaches Writing at City College. She worked as an actress and psychotherapist until making writing her priority. Her stories, essays, poems, and translations have appeared with W.W. Norton, *The New York Times, [sic], 138journal, Promethean, Epiphany, The Absinthe Literary Review, Dimension2* and several German newspapers.

J. J. Steinfeld is a fiction writer, playwright, and poet living in Charlottetown, Prince Edward Island, Canada. He has published a novel, *Our Hero in the Cradle of Confederation* (Pottersfield Press), nine short story collections, the previous three by Gaspereau Press—*Should the Word Hell Be Capitalized?, Anton Chekhov Was Never in Charlottetown,* and *Would You Hide Me?*—and a poetry collection, *An Affection for Precipices* (Serengeti Press).

Dorothy Stone, a retired teacher, is happily finding time for her own writing. Nominated for two Pushcart Prizes, her chapbook *Discovery Age* came out in 2007. Her poems, essays, memoir, and stories have appeared in such outlets as *Atlanta Review, The Formalist, Light, The Boston Globe, The Southern Poetry Review,* and *The Writing Group Book.* Her husband, also a writer, died last year. Her daughter and family help fill the void.

Patricia Sullivan has been published in the Suburban Diary feature of the *Boston Globe* newspaper. She won an honorable mention from *ByLine Magazine* for her poem "Celebrating Gracie." She is a member of LLARC (Lifelong Learning at Regis College) in Weston, Mass. Mother of five, grandmother of seven, she is retired and lives with her husband in North Billerica, Massachusetts.

Sylvie Terespolski's writings have included magazine articles that have appeared in *Insights, Main Line Magazine, The English Journal,* op-eds in the *Philadelphia Inquirer,* and a short story published in *Reconstructionist.* She has works in perpetual progress that include three plays and a novel currently titled *The Jew and the Pope.*

Don Thackrey spent his formative years on farms and ranches in the Sandhills of the Nebraska prairie, and most of his verse reflects that experience. He now lives in Dexter, Michigan, where he is retired from teaching and administering at the University of Michigan. He published prose during his university years, including a book on Emily Dickinson, but has only recently begun submitting verse for publication.

Sondra Zeidenstein's poems have been published in journals and anthologies, and in a chapbook collection entitled *Late Afternoon Woman. A Detail in that Story* is her first book, *Resistance* is her second. She is editor of *A Wider Giving: Women Writing after a Long Silence* and *Family Reunion: Poems about Parenting Grown Children,* and publisher of Chicory Blue Press, a small literary press (<www.chicorybluepress.com>) that focuses on writing by older women.

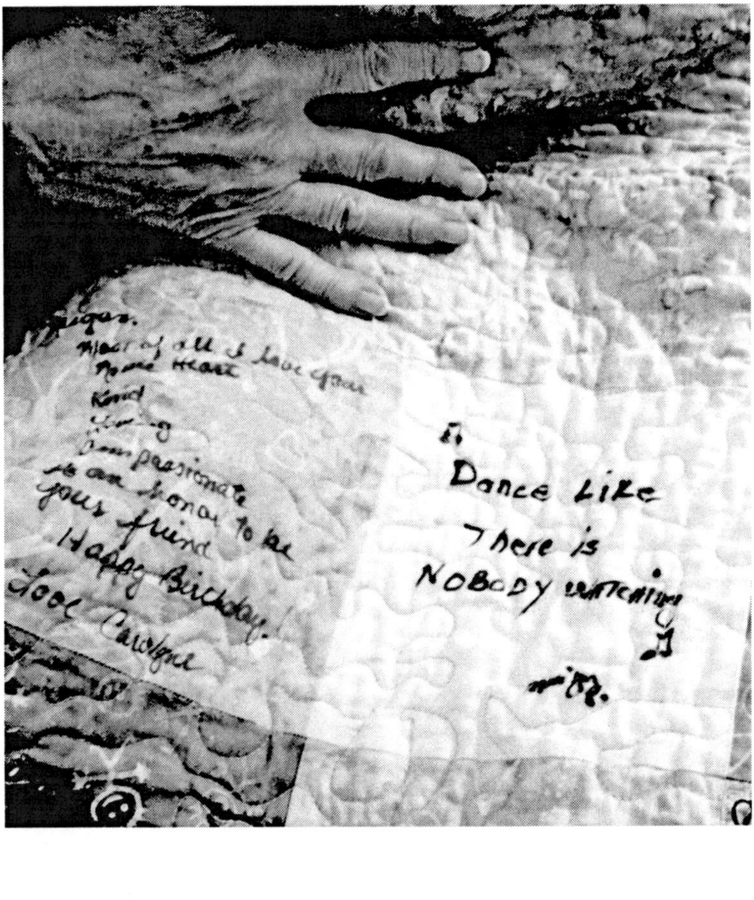
Compassionate
your friend
Happy Birthday
Dance Like
There is
NOBODY watching

ACKNOWLEDGEMENTS

Lois Barr's "Botanic Garden Waltz" was published in *Collage*.

William Borden's "Everything New" and "Creamy Love Pasta" first appeared in *Re-Imagining*. "The Snipe's Death-Defying Fall of Love" appeared in *Art Word Quarterly*.

Patricia Brodie's "Roots" was first published in her chapbook *The American Wives Club*; "Tanka" was first published in *Rattlesnake Review*.

Maureen Tolman Flannery's "The Last Time" was published in *Slant*.

Myrna Goodman's "A Good Man Is Hard to Find" appeared in *Desire Path* (Toadlily Press, 2005).

Grey Held's "Things Breaking in the House" was first published in *Sahara*.

Christina Lovin's "Photograph, 1975" first appeared at *Best Poem: A Poetry Journal*.

Mary O'Dell's "Garden Time" has appeared previously in *Passager*.

Carl Palmer's "Senior Moment" appeared previously in *La Fenetre "Reflections"*; "Her Candle" in *The Taj Mahal Review*; "Her New Room" in *Lucidity Magazine*.

Joyce Richardson's "Meet Me in Spoleto" originally appeared in *Best Ohio Poems of 2003*.

Elisavietta Ritchie's "One Wedding Night" was first published in *Kalliope* and "For a Jealous Suitor, Getting On" in *Amelia*. Both are reprinted in her book *Elegy For the Other Woman* (Signal Books, 1996).

Frank Salvidio's poems are reprinted from *Common Ground Review*.

Cynthia Sample's "The Prayer Diary of Doreen Newton" previously appeared in *Between the Lines*.

Wayne Scheer's "The Flowers on Bloom Street" was previously published in *Riverwalk Journal*.

Ada Jill Schneider's poems are reprinted from her book *Behind the Pictures I Hang* (Spinner Publications, Inc., 2007).

Lucille Gang Shulklapper's "And What Importance Do I Have in the Courtroom of Oblivion?" was first published by Ginninderra Press.

Anna Steegmann's "Hans in Luck" was first published in *Promethean*.

J.J. Steinfeld's "It Is Your Ninetieth Summer, You Tell Me" is from his book *An Affection for Precipices* (Serengeti Press, 2006).

Dorothy Stone's "Tethered" appeared in *REAL*; "Twenty Twenty" and "The Man in the Hotel Lutetia" in her chapbook *Discovery Age* (Autumn Light Press).

Sondra Zeidenstein's "Another Country" was first published in *Moondance*.

Photographs by Heather Tosteson.

Photograph of George's bench was generously contributed by Phyllis Langton.

EDITORS

MEGAN LILLER KRIVCHENIA is the mother of five amazing children and sixteen astonishing grandchildren. She did her undergraduate studies at Case University in Cleveland, OH and at Marietta College in Marietta, OH. She received her graduate degree fron Ohio University in Athens, OH. Megan is a retired family therapist and currently works as a mediator with people who are parenting separately. She resides in Williamstown, WV.

NANCY PELLETIER WYMOND is the author of a novel, *The Rearrangement* (MacMillan, 1986); short stories, including one in *Best American Short Stories*; poetry, and a play. Before retirement she was a professor of English at West Virginia University at Parkersburg, as well as chairman of the Humanities Department. She received a Masters in Creative Writing from Ohio University and has been a fellow at VCCA and the Ossabaw Island Project. The mother of four children, six grandchildren, and two great grandchildren, she lives in Marietta, Ohio, with her husband Louis Wymond.

EDITORS/PUBLISHERS

HEATHER TOSTESON, is the author of *Visible Signs* and *Hearts as Big as Fists*, and, most recently, *God Speaks My Language, Can You?*. She has received a Nation/Discovery prize for her poetry and fellowships for poetry, fiction, and photography from MacDowell, Yaddo, VCCA, and Hambidge. She holds a M.F.A. in Creative Writing (UNC-Greensboro) and Ph.D. in English and Creative Writing (Ohio University). She is founder and co-director of Universal Table and Wising Up Press.

CHARLES BROCKETT, having worked from an early age in a small book bindery co-owned by his father, is delighted by his second career as a book publisher—and co-director of Universal Table. He has written two well received books on Central America and numerous social science journal articles. A political science professor, he is a recipient of several Fulbright and National Endowment for the Humanities awards. His Ph.D. is from UNC-Chapel Hill. He lives in Atlanta.

See our booklist and calls for submissions for new anthologies
www.universaltable.org
wisingup@universaltable.org

Printed in the United States
204162BV00003B/1-102/P